# KINGDOM

JEREMY RANDOLPH
# KINGDOM

Winter Night Publishing

©2006

JEREMY RANDOLPH
# KINGDOM

**Kingdom.** Copyright © 2006 by Jeremy Randolph.

Printed and bound in the United States of America. All rights reserved. No part of this book may be reproduced in any form or by any electronic, mechanical, written, or other means including retrieval systems or information storage without permission in writing from the publisher and author.

Published by Winter Night Publishing. Nashville, Tennessee

First Edition.

Visit our Web site at WinterNightPublishing.com

This book is a work of fiction. All characters, places, names, and incidents either are products of the author's imagination or are used fictitiously. Any resemblance to any persons living or dead, locales, or actual events, is entirely coincidental.

Edited by Bethany Holmes/Maureen Neuroth
Interior Design: Jeremy Randolph
Cover Illustration: Jeremy Randolph
Author Photo: John Chastain

International Standard Book Number: 0-9725148-1-3

For all that I love, dear Lord, who have long since passed away...

# Part I
## The End

# Chapter One

It was summer, warm and perfect, with her things arranged on the bed because she was too weak to get up. There was the sound of a clock, the constant snap of forward motion he would always associate with pain. Beyond this the silence, the pale scent of medication and the unspoken truth that nothing was forever, not even her.

Arielle lay with her face to the ceiling, the smallest hint of a smile etched on her tired face. There was morphine in the bottle beside the bed and two of the red caplets swimming in her blood. Her once blond hair was soaked with the sweat of pain and the veins beneath her pallid skin ran like blue rivers across her face. She looked over at her brother and tried to smile.

Jonathan remembered the face he'd known, so different than the one looking up at him now. A face full of beauty and life, perfect in his limited understand of what life was. The memory took him back to when he'd known nothing of cancer, to a time when he was just a boy moving through the world. They'd grown into summer that year, laughing as the season fell down around them. The August landscape blazed green as they'd made their way down the empty street. Arielle was turning fifteen. Her hair pulled into a pony tail to keep it out of her face with no hint of the sickness growing inside her. She smiled easy and moved the same. Jonathan followed behind her, a boy hardly past ten.

The crashing of the approaching storm's first thunder echoed and Arielle turned her head towards the window. The movement made her sick but the change in view was refreshing. She had resigned herself to the fact she wouldn't make it through the night. There would be no more day for her to gaze upon. Once the light had gone and the darkness came there would be calm. She was going down this road alone.

She smiled up at her mother. In the world without her, it was coming, a place of dark forgetfulness with no back secrets to share. They would pass beyond each other, lives crossing lives. Arielle turned her eyes towards her brother and tried to speak.

It was hard to keep from crying and he was trying to be strong, the way she had always been with him. Sitting beside her, the terror of what it meant stole through him again. Arielle saw this and tried to reach her hand to him.

"It's okay, little brother."

He reached to her, finding the cold fingers and feeling anger rise at the thought of losing her.

"Don't forget what I told you," she whispered.

The memory that came hurt him. "I promise."

She smiled and for a moment he could see her as she used to be. "Take care of mama."

Jonathan tried to fight back tears but when Arielle squeezed his hand they spilled forth. She pulled him to her and he allowed himself to be hugged. He could feel the bones in her chest and wanted to trade places with her, wanted to change everything, but he could do nothing but cry.

They lay that way for an eternity, the animated rhythm of her breathing, hitching from time to time. If he let go, he knew he may never get to experience the sensation again, so he held on until she gently pushed him back.

"Mama?"

Their mother emerged from the shadows. "Yes, baby."

"Could you and daddy sit with me?"

Beyond the open window, the rain brought the scent of wet air. In its thickness Arielle's breathing began to labor. After an hour the fear she'd done so well holding back began to show. When she whispered four words in the silence of the room, Jonathan thought he would go mad with helplessness. "I'm not ready, mama."

Jonathan wondered how it had come to this. Only months before the sun had been at their backs. He and Arielle heading down Baker Street, laughing about nothing and taking in everything. The large sycamores lining the sidewalk cast shadows, giving slight relief from the scorching heat. They crossed onto Gideon's Circle and continued down until the road gave way to woods. Past these was Harbor Creek which emptied from the dam upstream. It had been raining for three days and the water was high. They could walk across without getting their knees wet most days but that wouldn't be the case today. Arielle stepped in wincing at the coolness.

"Be careful Johnny, current's fast."

At its deepest, it was to her waist and she held her shirt up trying to step where she knew it was shallowest. Jonathan followed her. She could hear him coming and turned once to check on him. The water was two inches above his waist but he didn't seem to be in any trouble. She climbed up on the other side and watched, ready to help if need be.

When they were both on the bank, they passed through a thicket of trees and onto flat green land. The blades of grass lay down with the wind. They stuck their hands out like airplanes and let their fingers dance through the tops of it. In the center of the field was an abandoned structure from the days when the land was a plantation. They made their way slow, talking about the coming school year and Jonathan's birthday. He would be eleven soon.

The structure or "their place", as Jonathan called it, was disheveled to the point of collapse with dry grey wood and a leaning roof. The interior wasn't as bad as the outside, protected from the elements by the limited shelter the walls and room still provided. Arielle had done her best to clean and repair anything she could since first discovering the place two years earlier. She'd had a fight with her mother over something stupid, something she couldn't even remember now, and had crossed the creek meaning to hide out until dark. She'd never realized there was anything actually on the other side and she'd fallen in love with the place at once.

Now inside with Jonathan, she pried up the floor board. She extracted her notebooks and set them aside, reaching back in for Jonathan's charcoals. The boy took them, humbled by the soft black marks they left on her fingers, and scurried across to the doorway. Arielle took her spot next to the window and gave him a smile. Their minds became their reality. Jonathan scanned the interior of their place then averted his gaze to the field trying to locate a subject. He spotted a rogue tree knocked down by some long ago storm. With quick strokes, he began to sketch its edges.

Arielle watched from her perch. He wasn't a Picasso yet, but he was getting better. Each picture showed more detail than the ones before. She was glad he'd found solace in something other than her company.

She began to write. The words came as they always did, filling page after page with her thoughts. She'd finished three others notebooks which still lay hidden beneath the floor. The one she held now had been bought on a whim while visiting her grandmother. It was on that trip she'd first began to feel sick and she'd spent most of the trip in bed.

"If I'd only known then," she wrote, "Jonathan has no idea. I feel bad about that. Mama says we can't tell him yet. It'll just make him sad. I'd like to let him know, but I suppose she's right. We had a great breakfast this morning, toast and eggs. Thank goodness it didn't make me sick. Sometimes eggs really eat into me. Got to thinking about things today. I saw this woman on the television that was pregnant. Her stomach was so huge, I couldn't believe it! She and her husband were showing off the new baby room to their parents. It made me sad because I'm not going to have that. It'll make mama sad too, I think, no grandbabies from her oldest. It's getting harder for me to stay strong. I put up a front for everybody but I'm very afraid. I feel so alone sometimes. The doctors keep telling me to hold out hope, but I think they're putting on their own front. I've overhead mama crying about me. I think they know something I don't."

"Arielle, could you throw me another piece."

She leaned over and plucked a charcoal from the box beside her. "You've already used up that one?"

"This tree has this big tear down the side, I had to push hard to get it the way I wanted."

By afternoon, the sky was turning purple. Long

tufts of white stretched lazy across it, vying for the horizon. Jonathan brought his picture over to get her opinion. She looked at it, still amazed at the level of talent he had so young, and wrapped it with her notebook.

"You keep drawing like that and I'll be visiting you in Rome."

They didn't hurry home, electing to walk slow and let the sun go down. Crickets singing, frogs croaking, green leaves rustling in the ebbing wind. Arielle closed her eyes and tried to soak up the feeling. Jonathan ran along in front of her, throwing rocks at street signs.

They arrived home wet from the creek. They changed their clothes and came down for dinner. Their father was working late so it would just be the three of them. With steaming food in front of them, each joined hands for grace. The sound of their mother's voice was soothing as it filled the kitchen.

"Lord, bless this food we are about to receive. Thank you for the days you have given us, and grant us many more to come. In your name we pray, Amen."

The three talked for awhile about school and chores as the food was passed and the drinks poured. No mention was made of their activities beyond the woods. Once the table was clear and the dishes put away, they retired to the den.

Jonathan lay in bed staring at the ceiling. The longer he went, the more things he would see. One minute there was a forest, the next, people. Then the people would be gone replaced by mountains.

He woke three hours later and made his way down the hall to the bathroom. The floor was cold and the need to relieve himself intense. He lifted the lid and found blood on the rim, blood in the water, and blood on the floor. Frightened he ran to his parent's room and found the light on and the bed made. Downstairs he found a note on the kitchen table.

"Dear Jon, Arielle got sick and we had to take her to the hospital. If you need anything, just call grandma. Mom."

He sat alone in the kitchen until the sun rose, his mind reeling. What was wrong with her? Why didn't they get him up? There were no answers to these questions; only scenarios which he found made his mouth dry and his heart race. When he'd worked himself into near panic the front door opened. His father came in carrying a small sack.

"Hey buddy, you decide to wake up?"
"Dad, what happened to Arielle?"
"She got sick this morning."
"Is she okay?"
"She's fine, you hungry?"
"A little."
"I brought some biscuits."

He emptied the contents onto the table.

"Why don't you fix us a couple glasses of juice?"
"Is mama still at the hospital?"
"Yes."
"Are they coming home soon?"
"Soon as the doctor says its okay."

They didn't return until well past noon. Jonathan was upstairs when he heard the front door open and ran down the stairs.

"Mom, is she okay?"

"She's a little tired."

He scooted past her into the den. "Hey sis, you okay?"

"Got a little sick this morning."

"I know, I woke up and everybody was gone."

"Well you're a big kid, you don't need guidance."

It made him laugh. "We gonna go back to the field today?"

"I think I'm gonna stay in. I'm pretty tired."

They sat together for the rest of the afternoon, Jonathan watching television, Arielle dozing. She would wake coughing and have to go to the bathroom. Jonathan could remember thinking she had caught a bad cold. It wasn't until three weeks later that he learned the truth.

They had gone to their place. Jonathan was working on a raven and Arielle was writing in her notebook. When she called him over he could tell something was wrong, her tone wasn't right.

"Johnny, could you come over here for a second?"

Jonathan made a wide sweep across the page and sat his charcoal down. "What's up?"

"I'm sick Johnny."

"Do you need to go home?"

"No. Listen, mom and dad don't want me telling you this, but I think you should know."

"Okay."

"Last time I went to the doctor they found something they can't fix."

"Are you gonna be alright?"

"No."

"What do you mean?"

"There's nothing they can do to fix me."

Jonathan was silent. "Are you going to die?"

She didn't speak, she didn't need to.

The first ghost of a tear rose in his eyes. "How long until it happens?"

"They're not sure. Month, maybe two."

He couldn't breath. "Are you scared?"

"Yes."

Jonathan put his arms around her and hugged. "I don't want you to go."

Arielle stroked the top of his head. "I know you don't."

Beyond the doorway, the groan of thunder came and raindrops began to tap the roof. In the fading daylight, the shadows grew long across the floor. The raven he'd been working on drifted across it, small specs of water distorting its face.

At dinner, Jonathan wouldn't speak. When questioned on his silence he said he was worn out, ready for bed. When he finally got to it, he turned out the light and lay on the floor. With his feet propped on a box, he stared out at the drifting moon.

She couldn't die. It wasn't fair. He waited in the dark until all the doors were closed and the lights extinguished before putting on his jeans and slipping into the hall. The only illumination came from the bathroom nightlight and he didn't have to wonder why it was on. Crossing to the stairs he could hear the soft breathing of his mother. They hadn't wanted him to know, hadn't wanted him to worry. They had no right.

He descended the stairs, crossed to the front door, and exited into the night. He ran to the sidewalk, gaining speed as he went. Dogs barked as he flew by, the harsh slapping of his feet echoing through the night.

His side hurt and his lungs burned but he kept going. When he reached the gate surrounding St. Andrew's cemetery, he jumped, landing in the courtyard. The large windows of the church glared down at him. He grabbed a low hanging branch and ascended into an ancient tree. He climbed until the branches began to bow and the wind was hard in his face. He found his favorite perch and stopped climbing.

Sixty feet above the churchyard gave him a view of the town. The stone garden below stretched out into darkness. Arielle's face swam up in his mind and the tears he'd concealed spilled forth. He rocked back and forth, swaying with the tree in the evening wind, wanting only to keep things the way they were.

Three days later brought his birthday and the family spent it together opening presents and eating cake. When the party was over Arielle asked him to come with her to the field, it had been days since she'd felt good enough to go and Jonathan jumped at the chance. They made a point not to mention her sickness and they had to move a little slower but Jonathan didn't mind. It was time well spent.

Arielle sat down in her spot and asked him to get the stuff from the floor. Jonathan didn't want to. She saw his displeasure and smiled.

"Just do it for me this once."

He pulled back the board, his mind hating the idea, and saw something he didn't recognize. Turning, he saw Arielle smiling back at him.

"Go on, get it out," she said.

It was heavy, wrapped in green paper with a silver bow.

"Bring it over here," she said and patted the floor next to her.

When both were ready, he dove in. The paper peeled back revealing a wooden box. Jonathan turned it over and found a small gold plate.

"To my baby brother. Love always, Arielle."

Flipping the latch, he opened it. Inside was lush green velvet. Across the top were long pieces of charcoal. Every shade was there, from white to dark black. It was the most beautiful thing Jonathan had ever seen.

Arielle basked in the look on her brother's face.

"Where did you find this?"

"I didn't. I had it made for you."

"You did? It must have cost a fortune."

"Well I've been saving since I was your age."

"Not your special fund?"

"Yes."

"No Arielle, I can't take this."

"Jon listen to me. That money was for my dream. I don't think I'm gonna have time to do all the things I wanted so I wanted to do something special for you. This is our place, our secret. I don't ever want you to forget. When I'm gone, I don't want you to stop coming here."

"I couldn't come here without you."

"I don't want you to stop because of me. I don't ever want you to stop, promise me."

He hesitated.

"Jon."

He didn't want to think about coming here without her. She was still waiting for his reply and the look on her face broke his heart.

"I promise."

For a moment neither spoke.

"I'll tell you a secret about that box."

"What?"

"The wood's from the floorboard."

Jonathan looked over and saw a board was missing. "Why did you use that?"

"So no matter where you go, you will always have a piece of this place, a piece of our time here."

"I'm scared, Arielle."

"I'm scared too."

It would be the last time they were there together. They admitted Arielle to the hospital for aggressive chemo-therapy the following week. She stayed there for four more before coming home to die. The whole time she was gone Jonathan stayed away from the field. It wouldn't be right without her.

The coughing became harder. Jonathan could tell how bad it hurt her. Arielle's eyes were fixed on her mother and she was trying to speak.

"I love you guys."

Jonathan watched his sister drift in and out of sleep. As midnight neared, she began to whimper. Jonathan felt the hand holding his tighten and tried to comfort her. The soft white of her fingers were cold upon him. Then without warning they released. His mother registered the change and began to speak to her daughter. Jonathan watched in horror as she began to smile. Something behind them had caught Arielle's attention. He turned but saw nothing. When his gaze returned, she let out a final breath. The hand holding her mother's slipped out.

His mother began to chant the word, no, in continuous growing fervor. As the sound began to peak, Jonathan felt himself coming apart. Everything began unraveling deep in his head. His father scooped Arielle into his arms and began to rock her. Large tears streamed down his face. Jonathan had never seen his father cry, and the sight of it broke him.

He tore from the room. The darkness of the hallway disoriented him and he went down. Climbing to his feet, he continued to stumble towards the stairs. He exited the front door mindless of the pelting rain.

There was no traffic on the tiny street. Distant thunder groaned across the world. Fits of lightning danced. He fell in their front yard and felt the water seep into his clothes. The leaves above him danced in the torrent wind. Jonathan closed his eyes and saw her laughing, the joy in her face made his stomach clench. He threw up and passed out.

A short time later a hand was shaking him. The rain had stopped but it was still dark. Struggling to open his eyes he heard his father's voice.

"Come inside, John."

Jonathan tried to sit up. For a moment he thought the whole thing had been a dream. "Arielle?"

"Let's get inside."

His mind was racing, but no clear thought would come. The memory felt like a dream, taunting him with promises that it hadn't been real, he was still safe asleep in his bed and nothing had changed. Then reality fell in on him and he began to cry. His father lifted him into his arms, mindless of the water and foulness.

The two went back into the house where they found his mother wrapped in a blanket on the living room phone. Jonathan's father carried him past her into their bedroom. "Take a quick shower; I'll bring you some pajamas."

Jonathan did.

Afterwards, he lay in his parent's bed and saw a pair of men roll a stretcher into her room. A little while later they came back out with a black bag resting on top of it. He knew that she was in there, but couldn't get his mind around the reality of it.

He'd expected the whole world to end, or that some great change would cement the fact that she had gone, and yet the air conditioner was still running, the lights in the house were still on, and the bed he sat on still held the familiar warmth he'd always known. This place of deep comfort where nothing bad would ever be able to get to him.

Then the door was closed by his father in an attempt to block his view, but it didn't matter what they did, the scene was now a part of him.

# Chapter Two

Jonathan began sixth grade as an only child spending most of his days alone. The world in his head was much better than the one his body occupied. In that world Arielle was well, the color in her cheeks full. In this world, old women said, "I'm so sorry." People he didn't know would ask him if he was okay. Kids in his class who'd barely spoken three words to him in the past came to get the morbid details from a kid who had seen death. They'd mask it with conversations about baseball or movies but it would always come back to the same.

"Were you there when it happened?"

"What was it like?"

"Did she scream?"

Jonathan didn't like to favor them with a reply. When the questions came he would be up, walking across the playground hands in his pocket, head down. It went on like that for awhile, questions without answers, but the constant barrage eventually wore him down enough that he began to give small details to calm the questions. Yes he had been there, no she didn't scream. Each time he talked about her it made him feel dirty. Arielle was a person and Arielle was gone.

Isolation wasn't wasted at home either. After the funeral his mother stayed in her room for days. Jonathan would arrive home to an empty house, the curtains always drawn and no matter how warm it was outside, inside it was freezing. With his father at work, he didn't have anyone to talk to. Arielle had always been his companion and it was a rare occasion when she wouldn't have something exciting for them to do.

The only thing he had left of her now was sitting under a weather floorboard in the center of a field and he couldn't bring himself to go out there. The thought of walking all that way alone, of crossing through the water without her to guide him, to cross the length of the field and climb the steps into the familiarity of their place tore at his heart. If he went and became accustomed to her being gone, then the initial feeling of going there would be replaced by one without her. He found things had already begun to move in a forgetful pattern. Pictures were moved, conversations now skated around subjects that may lead into painful memories. Everyone was broken and the normalcy of the world was gone. Evolution was at hand and he wanted no part of it.

The days passed as winter neared. Jonathan continued to sit alone, watching the world as it passed. With the weather turning colder he began to worry more and more about their things being out in the elements. He had promised her that he would continue to go to their place but he was unsure that he would be able. Perhaps he wouldn't be able to go for a long time, months, maybe years, and he knew that even with all their repair efforts and precautions the small room was old. If it were to fall, or was torn down with their things in it he would never forgive himself. He reached beside the couch and got his shoes.

Five minutes later he was out of the gate and running hard. He crossed Baker Street onto Gideons Circle. Houses rushed by, staring at him as he went. He crossed from pavement onto grass then into the underbrush at the edge of the creek. He stood for a moment watching the water lap the edge of the bank before scooping a rock from the mud and tossing it in. The thump was deep. Arielle never let him cross when it was so deep but he wasn't waiting.

Wading out he felt pressure against his legs and struggled to keep his balance. He flirted with the idea of turning back but the thought of having to go through this again stopped him. If it got too deep, he'd swim for it.

Gathering his will he began moving. It only took a second for the current to begin pushing. Each step moved him a few down and not across. Three more steps and the water was up to his neck. The cold was unforgiving and his teeth were beginning to chatter. Fear took hold as he got to the center and felt the rocks beneath his feet start slipping.

When it got too deep to touch he held his breath and lunged towards the side. The current grabbed him and began pulling him down river. He felt panic grab hold as he struggled to breath. Paddling as hard as he could he hit something hard, recognized it as a tree limb, and began using it to pull himself across.

He rolled onto the bank, gasping. The wind cut through his soaked clothes and he began to shiver. Hugging himself, he rolled over and began wading through the foliage. As he came out from the cover of trees the moon poked out laying hues of light across the field. He could see the shelter, shadowed by moonlight and seemingly unharmed. He was overcome by a sudden need to look away from it and did. Arielle wasn't with him and it felt wrong.

"She's never gonna be with you again and everything feels wrong," a voice deep in his head whispered.

The wind was harder in the open and it got him moving. The familiar markings of the windows became apparent the closer he came. Most had been broken years before. He ascended the stairs and recognized many of the pictures he'd drawn still hanging on the walls. His favorites were lying beneath the floor with his box. Going to it, he pried the floor up. The moon shed little light but Jonathan could see the soft cover of Arielle's notebooks. Beside them was the box she'd made him. He brought out the notebooks first, setting them on the ground. He picked the box up next, loving the feel of it. The drawings were the last to be extracted and he took a moment to look through them. The site of many brought back painful memories and he set them aside.

Arielle's notebooks were the next to be inspected. There were three in all, two pink and one grey. Jonathan saw all but the last twenty or so pages were written on, both front and back. He didn't think she'd mind him looking now when nothing inside could hurt her. He flipped to a random page and let his eyes take in the familiar script. Indentions in paper made by her, things that could never be replaced, sitting forgotten for so long he felt guilt slip her arms around him. He began to read, the sick emptiness in him building.

"It's hot out here today. Jonathan's over there working on a ladybug. Says it keeps looking at him, so he needs to draw it. I like how he says he "needs" to draw it as though he has no choice in the matter. It's peaceful out here, not like the house last night. Mom and dad were fighting about something. I could hear dad yelling something about money and wasteful something or other all the way upstairs. I don't know why they get so mad at each other."

Jonathan turned the page.

"Started feeling sick this morning, we've only got two more weeks of school left and I can't be missing any days. If I'm lucky, I won't have to take all of my exams. Jonathan doesn't know how good he's got it. He just told me he hoped mom was cooking chicken tonight. I'd like to eat some chicken too, but my stomach might not let me."

Jonathan closed the notebook and set it aside. Seeing her words made his heart ache. He leaned back against the wall and stared into the dark. The wind shuttered through the cracks in the walls. He was freezing and tired but it would take awhile for the creek to subside. When he fell asleep, no dreams greeted him. He waded in the perfect black until the first light of morning broke.

When he reached the creek he was thankful to see the water had dropped. He managed to cross holding their things above his head without much problem. On the way home, he tried to walk out of sight.

Once in his room, he set what he'd brought from the field on his bed. He wasn't sure where to hide it. He went through many scenarios, most ending with his mother finding the notebooks and reading them. He tried a variety of locations and was attempting to find a place at the rear of his closet when he got an idea.

There was a small pocketknife on his dresser and he picked it up. Returning to the closet, he pushed back his clothes and unfolded the blade. Trying to be as quiet as possible, he began sawing. He continued on the other three sides until a piece of drywall the size of a shoe box fell out. The space behind it was large enough to fit everything in. He took his drawings and

Arielle's notebook and placed them inside. The box he kept out, putting it as far back as he could on the closet floor. He set the piece of drywall back in place then did his best to cover it.

When he got up around noon and came downstairs no one was there. A plate of biscuits sat on the table so he grabbed two and headed to the porch.

The sun shone bright warming the air. Sitting Indian style, he watched the parade of cars roll by. Even with the constant noise it felt quiet.

"What are you doing?"

The voice startled him. Looking up he saw their neighbor, Bailey Hazelwood.

"Eatin' breakfast."

"Little late for breakfast isn't it?"

"I suppose."

Bailey Hazelwood had lived in Morning Ridge for the better part of his life. A veteran of the Second World War, he was prone to talk about the old times. Arielle loved to stop by his house whenever she could. She said his stories were "fascinating."

"Your ma around?"

"No sir, I'm not sure where she is."

"Any idea what time she'll be back."

"Not really."

Bailey considered. "Well, Abbey wanted me to drop off these tomatoes."

Jonathan walked to the gate and took the bag. "I can take 'em."

"It's good to see you outside, not good for a boy your age to be cooped up."

Jonathan let the bag hang at his side. "Yeah."

Bailey grew reflective. "How you doing these days?"

Jonathan shrugged. "I'm okay I guess."

"Rough times?"

"Yes sir."

"Well, good times will come around too. Life's funny that way. Tell your ma there's more where those came from."

"I will."

"You feel free to stop by anytime. I'll get Abbey to make us some lemonade and I'll tell you about the time I was in the war." He rustled Jonathan's hair and headed back down the street.

When his mother pulled up a short time later he was still on the porch. She'd walked past him carrying two bags of groceries before he got motivated to help. They made three trips until the car was empty.

"Mr. Hazelwood brought some tomatoes by."

"Did he? Where are they?"

"Out on the porch."

"Well go get them and get washed up."

His mother had started cooking again. For a few weeks they ate only food brought by family and neighbors. The alternate taste of strangers food lent to the ever increasing differences his life was taking on. When she'd finally started, the familiarity in it, however small, was appreciated.

After dinner, Jonathan sat alone in his room. The closet stared out at him, but he didn't dare chance it. When he heard his parent's door close he relaxed a little. He'd made up his mind to read one passage at a time until it got too hard, or he felt he should stop. He would pace himself, no more than one page a night, and savor what little he had left of his sister.

Pulling the flashlight from his dresser, he opened the closet. The hole he'd cut hadn't been disturbed and it came loose with a few jiggles. With it out of the way he could see the pink cover of her notebook. Sliding it out he relished its feel.

Opening to the first page, he read her name. It was scrawled in swooping letters across the entire front page. Under it was a date. Arielle's birthday, two years earlier. Flipping the page back, he gazed on her familiar script in dark blue ink. The top of the page said, Saturday, May 12th.

"I'm starting this journal as a way of remembering. I can't remember much of what's happened in my life so far, except maybe the big stuff. I want to remember it all, every silly little moment. Patty has one that she let me see, but she wouldn't let me read it. I thought it was a great idea. So where to start? Okay, it's Saturday. I'm home with my little brother Jonathan. He's nine. My name is Arielle Constance Murray. I'm thirteen. I live in a town called Morning Ridge. Tonight we had baked potatoes and carrots for dinner. Dad helped make the roast. He's getting better at cooking. It was mom's idea to teach him. He kept complaining that he didn't have anything to eat when she worked late. I'm in the seventh grade; I guess I should put that in here. It's a new school and I like most of my teachers. I have a few friends that I've made since I've been there. My favorite class is science, my worst is math. There's supposed to be snow tonight or tomorrow so we might not have school. Jonathan is excited about the idea. I have a test that I've been studying for all day. If we don't go, I'll have to restudy. It's about ten o'clock now, and looking out the window I see the big tree in our front yard. It's moving back and forth pretty good so there must be a storm coming. I'm not sure what else to write right now. I need to go to sleep in case we do go to school tomorrow. This is Arielle Murray, signing off."

Jonathan closed the notebook. Part of him wanted to look for her, to go down the hall to her room and ask her why she hadn't come out in so long. She couldn't really be gone.

He climbed into bed. There was a magic missing. The innocence of life had been taken away. He became aware that nothing really mattered. In the end, everyone was going into the darkness. In the end, all would be done.

# Chapter Three

Christmas vacation came without her. As the world moved closer to the twenty-forth it began to fold in on itself. Windows began to glow with ornate trees. Bushes blazed with glowing reds and blues. Jonathan made his way down the aisle of the bus, listening to the lunatic excitement on the lips of every child, things they would do, what they had asked for, perfect and sheltered in the safety of the coming season. He climbed down the five steps, careful not to get caught up in the doors as they opened and stepped out onto the sidewalk. The bus thundered and pulled away taking with it the indistinguishable voices he himself was once lost in only the year before. All he wanted now was the simple quiet of his room.

By nightfall he'd been sitting at the window for hours. The snow had begun to fall, slow and accumulating, and though his eyes were focused on the window, he saw nothing but his thoughts. A group of older kids were playing in the streets below. There were two groups, one with two boys and another with three girls. The war between them was a white blur. One of the girls noticed him looking down and threw a snowball at his window. It exploded in white spray and brought Jonathan back to the world. She stuck out her tongue and was hit by an incoming ball. She screamed and ran after the boy who'd thrown it. She stopped long enough to scoop a handful of snow and launch it at her attacker. She hit the boy in the leg and he tripped over his feet falling face first into a drift along the sidewalk. The other kids erupted in laughter. The girl looked up at him again, winked, and then ran as vengeance came in another assault.

A simple need began to build in Jonathan. He crossed to his closet and opened the door. The box was still hidden in the shadows, unopened since he'd placed it there. The worn wood was smooth against his hands and he picked it up loving the feel. There was a tablet of paper in his desk and he brought it out.

The smell of charcoal was faint, the weight of the paper comforting. With a need he'd not felt in ages, he extracted a small piece and began to draw. At first the movements were stiff, then the part of his mind that controlled his gift took over. The image began to rise from the dark, a small shadow becoming a feature. With strange precision he began to move. Darkness began to lift accenting a nose. The girl outside continued to chase her opponents oblivious to the boy at the window.

Beneath the nose, a mouth was formed. Quick thrusts and cheekbones followed. When the shouting began to move down the street, the need for the scene was no longer necessary. It was behind his eyes like a photograph. He captured the trees with their sagging branches and ominous lines, brought the edges of the street along their stony path picking up each crack with strange detail. Long into the night he worked, sweat standing out on his forehead. Two pieces of charcoal lay broken beside him.

In the early hours of morning he fell back onto the floor, wiping his face and leaving smears across both cheeks. Staring into the ceiling he felt a sense of wholeness. The intensity had been replaced by silent calm. In its absence exhaustion closed over him. He fell asleep where he was, the picture he'd drawn lying finished beside him.

When he woke confused he realized he was still on the floor. Sitting up, he scanned for his picture and found it under his nightstand. He reached down and picked it up marveling at the image. It stared back at him, a photographic rendering of the girl captured in all her isolation. He could see the other kids too, but they didn't look real. There was a static to them, unfocused silhouettes caught in altered movements. There was something horrible about their positioning, something wrong, then his door opened and he pushed the paper behind him.

"Back on the floor again?" It was his mother.

Jonathan tried to answer but his heart was pounding, "Yeah."

"Well get up from there and come down, breakfast is getting cold."

Downstairs the kitchen was coated in a soft film of smoke. Steam rose from a bowl of scrambled eggs in the middle of the table. His father sat in front of them drinking a cup of coffee.

"Hey buddy, mom told me you were sleeping on the floor last night. Is your bed broken?"

"No sir, I was watching the snow and fell asleep."

"Well I hope you got some rest, we're going with you to church tonight."

"You decided to go?"

Jonathan decided after days of indecision that he would go on Christmas Eve. He mentioned his plans to his parents and they had assured him they thought he should go, but made no mention of accompanying him.

"Well, it's been awhile. I think it'd do us good." His father looked at his mother and she turned back to the dishes.

Jonathan and Arielle had gone every Christmas Eve whether their parents went or not. Arielle loved the Christmas songs and would sit as close as she could. As the organ rose she would sing with the congregation, the clarity of her voice soothing.

# KINGDOM

The service was at seven. Jonathan and his father were downstairs waiting by six thirty. Upstairs they could hear the woman of the house rustling around in the bathroom. When she finally came down, Jonathan was struck by how beautiful she looked. It had been awhile since she'd taken the time to get ready for anything.

They piled into the truck, elbow to elbow, the smell of his mother's perfume filling the cab. They rode through town talking of the latest news and changes. Jonathan's father told about the new products they were getting in at work. His mother said she'd heard a rumor that Jefferson's pharmacy was closing at the end of the season. Jonathan didn't like that idea. It was the best place for ice cream in the entire county.

They came down Jefferson Avenue and saw the church parking lot was almost full. Lights from swarming headlights circled down one isle and back up the other. Father Mason was sitting beneath the dim glow of the eves, a bible tucked in the crook of his arm. His spectacles caught the passing headlights and reflected them.

"Gonna have a full house tonight," his father said pulling the truck alongside the building. "Julia, you go ahead and get out, me and Jonathan will park."

His mother opened the door, bringing in the cold.

"Looks like we might have to walk a bit, you up for it?"

Jonathan nodded.

The only remaining spaces weren't spaces at all.

They were empty patches of grass adjacent to the asphalt. Twenty or so cars were already lined there, so his father pulled the truck in beside them.

"If we get a ticket, I'll tell them you were driving."

Julia Murray was waiting inside the doors where the cold of the wind was cut by the warmth of the church. Jonathan's father spoke to Father Mason as they passed. Beyond the man was the larger interior doors which opened on a roomful of people. The pews were packed with the occasional space along a few. Jonathan passed into the main room, walking beneath the choir settling in the roost above him.

The service began with a greeting. Father Mason thanked them all for coming, commenting on the new faces he saw. "Always good to see the Lord's house full."

Afterwards, Jonathan was more quiet than usual. The vacancy of his sister was wearing him down. They'd be in the church basement by now, eating cookies and drinking punch. His eyes were glazed and Father Mason had to say his name again. Jonathan felt his own father nudge him. When the dream cleared, he realized what was expected and shook the man's hand.

"I hope you enjoyed the service."

"Yes, sir."

The man nodded. "Have a merry Christmas."

Jonathan felt himself heading back into his mind. Arielle hovered in the air around him. He followed a few feet behind his parents to the car. They were talking in whispers about the food they had to cook, and what needed to be done before morning.

Everyone piled back into the truck. His mother snuggled in next to his father giving Jonathan the window seat. They managed to get out of the grass, but found traffic was stopped. Jonathan rested his head against the glass and stared at the families walking through the parking lot. There were children he'd played with running up and down the stairs of the church. They were brimming with the excitement only Christmas Eve can bring.

The ride home was filled with the same whispering voices. His parents found solace in talking of the old times. Jonathan found their stories of Christmas in college, before he was even born, comforting.

Once home, he excused himself and went upstairs. The light from the moon cast shadows along the floor. He left the light off and lay down, waiting for his parents to go to bed. When the last light went off, he rose and went to the closet.

"November 17th. Jonathan and I had an interesting experience today. There were some other kids hanging around our place. They were younger, closer to Jonathan's age than mine, but they still looked like trouble. Jonathan said he knew one of them and that the kid was a bully. Whatever the case, they got too close to the door so I jumped out onto the porch and screamed, "Get off my land!" They bolted like rabbits. Jonathan waited until they were gone before he would come out. I think the bigger kid scared him a little. Anyway, we had a good time of it after that."

Jonathan could still remember the way she'd run at the boys, arms up and flailing. He'd laughed to himself the next day at school when Russell Harris, the boy bully, swore the old man's widow had chased them with a shotgun.

He decided to read one more page as a Christmas present to himself.

"November 18th. There's a dance coming up at school but Eric hasn't asked me yet. I'm hoping he will. He's been acting kinda funny since the other day. He asked me why I seemed so tired all the time. I didn't want to tell him about being sick, but he kept pressing me. I'm not sure how he took it. He got really quiet and didn't say anything for awhile. It kinda hurt my feelings. Finally, he asked me if I was going to get better. I told him I hoped so, but I wasn't sure. I couldn't tell what he was thinking; he just kept looking at me. Before we could really get into it, his mom came home. We haven't really talked much since then, and if we do it's about the weather or something stupid. He hasn't kissed me either. I'm not sure if he's scared of me or what. I cried like a baby about it last night. I keep praying that everything will be okay with us again. I miss having him around."

Jonathan closed the book. The world was so far away. So many days were yet to come, so many different things to see and know. In his heart the darkness was swimming. It dawned on him that everything was dying. Through every shallow laugh, every wanted smile, the thing which made him live, was slipping out. He could hear the silence in the room, listening as if it knew what he was, and what he'd learned. He spent the rest of the night huddled beneath his covers, praying for sleep and finding none.

When the sun rose, he found his mother at the kitchen table staring out across the front yard. He could hear his father beating eggs somewhere out of view. In the living room, the Christmas tree blazed. There were presents stacked around it like offerings to some fragrant pine god.

The majority of the gifts were his, placed precariously around the wrapped ones. They were there, but they didn't matter. They were just a means to get his mind off of what was real. The entire room was full of the mystique of calmness. Yet to Jonathan, it was an empty reminder.

His parents came when they heard him rustling around. His mother put her arm around him. Jonathan tried to smile and hoped it looked more real than it felt. They began to pass gifts around. The sounds of ripping paper flooded their ears. His mother had bought him a new pair of boots. To her delight, they fit well. His father had bestowed him a watch, engraved with his initials and the words, "To my son." The biggest gift came last. It was a blue and silver bike, the one he'd asked for for his birthday. They hadn't had the money then and he knew they didn't have it now, but they were trying to help him back from where ever he was going.

Jonathan spent the rest of the morning riding it up and down Baker Street. The wind in his hair helped soothe the loneliness in his heart. As the houses raced by he realized something he hadn't before. What he knew as home had changed forever. The life that was, was as far from him as Arielle. He was going away from himself, and he wasn't sure he would ever come back. As the air of the town he'd been in his whole life filled his lungs, a distinct and unmistakable feeling of restlessness descended on him.

# Chapter Four

Bailey Hazelwood stepped onto the porch and lit a cigar. The smell wafted into his clothes giving him the ageless fragrance anyone who knew him recognized. Christmas was five months dead, leaving the earth to green. It was fair weather, and it suited him well. The humid summers of Morning Ridge were some of the worst in the county but they were still eons away as far as he was concerned.

Fragrant breezes blew down from Baker Street and what little hair he had blew in tangles as it did. He'd quit taking these walks during the winter, Abbey was sure he'd catch his death of cold, but now that summer was approaching Bailey wasn't concerned at the prospect. He'd get out a bit and see what there was to see.

The majority of the trip would be random, he didn't really have anywhere to go, and he hoped to air out some of the tension he'd been feeling. Things with Abbey were getting worse. It was strange to have her mind shorting out. One minute she'd be talking normal, the next she couldn't remember who she was. He knew it was the Alzheimer's. So far he hadn't felt any effects of the disease, but it seemed to him it got all the "old one's" eventually. When Abbey first started showing signs, he'd made her go to the doctor who confirmed what both suspected. He gave her some medicine to slow the onset and sent her home. That had been two years ago. Abbey wasn't forgetting things as bad, but she was growing increasingly hostile towards him.

They'd idle along having a fine conversation and she'd fly off the handle. It could follow an off sided comment about something small. "Noticed you changed the flowers out front, looks nice." or, "This is good meatloaf, better than last time." It had been over coffee this morning. She'd changed brands and he'd noticed.

He crossed Sixth Street and headed south. He found his mind going back to his youth a lot lately. He and Abbey were the only two left from that time of his life. With Abbey's progression, he was beginning to feel the end of himself following with it. All the old friends and family had passed. There was a huge world coming up behind him full of newness and vibrancy. He felt what it meant to be him was moving closer to the edge of oblivion. No man lived forever, but no man really thinks he'll die. He'd read that once somewhere, many years before, and even though he was aware he was breaking down, he always thought he'd see another day. Trick of the mind he supposed.

The thoughts were pushed away by the sound of peddling. He could hear the whooshing of tires and turned in time to see Jonathan Murray descending upon him. "Morning Jon." He said as the boy slid to a stop.

"Hello Mr. Hazelwood, whatcha doing way out here?"

"Taking a walk. What about you?"

"Oh, I was gonna go fishing."

Bailey looked at the bike then back at Jonathan. "Kind of hard to do without a pole isn't it?"

Jonathan smiled. "I said I was gonna go."

"Oh." Bailey gauged him, "Well what are you going to do now?"

"Nothing I guess, just ride around awhile."

"Well don't let me keep you from it."

Jonathan hopped back on his bike. "See you later."

Bailey raised his hand. Jonathan began to peddle and disappeared down the sidewalk.

The boy was acting odd in Bailey's opinion but it wasn't his business to judge. By mid-afternoon he'd walked out all his tension. He rounded the corner he saw Jonathan sitting outside his gate.

"You forget something?"

Jonathan looked down. "Sort of."

Bailey pulled up his pant legs and sat down beside him. "What's on your mind?"

"Did you know my sister well?"

"Arielle, yes. She'd come by sometimes and talk with Abbey and I."

"I read something once, I mean, well, I heard something once that I kinda wanted to ask you about."

Bailey found himself wondering again about the boy's mental state. "Okay."

Jonathan tried to gauge Mr. Hazelwood's face and found he couldn't. "Did you used to be a painter?"

Bailey regarded the question. "Once upon a time perhaps, though there are some who would say otherwise." Jonathan saw a smile light Bailey's face.

"What did you paint?" Jonathan asked.

"Kitchens, sometimes whole houses. I liked to do the insides more than the outsides."

Jonathan thought the man was being serious.

"No, I'm teasing you. I used to paint when I was a younger man, started when I was a few years older than you. We had these Okies...you know what an Okie is?"

"Yeah, I've read about them in history class."

"Well, my family back then was poor. Most of the food we had, we grew ourselves. My father had some acreage that the bank hadn't foreclosed on. The Okies would come to seed or pick vegetables. There wasn't enough work year round so we'd hire them as they passed through."

Bailey gazed across the street. "I started drawing first until I got pretty good at it, then my mother showed me how to make paint. We'd use skim milk from one of our cows, a bit of lime soap. I'd grind up the lime and mix a little water and milk in. Once I got it thick enough, I'd separate it into a few different containers. I'd use what I could to color it, mostly berries when I could find some or rust from the pump handle. You'd be surprised what you could use to for color. At any rate, I used some cow hair to make brushes. They weren't the greatest, but they did what they were meant to."

"What sort of stuff did you paint?"

"Started out with simple things, old buckets, chickens, things like that. I was your age when I first tried to paint a living person. I'd done two from photographs, one of my mother, the other of an old man. It would be the beginning of the end of my life as a painter."

"Did the picture turn out bad?"

"No, it was one of the best I'd done up to that point."

"So what happened?"

"Life did."

Above them, the trees began rustling. Their shadows crawled across the asphalt painting the world in grey. Bailey sat with a look of vacancy. He wasn't in the present anymore, he'd slipped back into the heat of California, to the smells of the fields and the voice of his father. "My God boy, what did you do?"

The voice of a mother brought him back to the world.

"Sounds like someone's looking for you."

Jonathan turned in the direction of the voice. "Yeah, I told her I'd be back by twelve."

Bailey looked at his watch. "You're late by about an hour."

Jonathan picked up his bike. "I'll see ya."

Bailey got back up and headed towards his own house. Inside he found Abbey knitting in the den seemingly in better spirits.

"I've made a bit of stew if you'd like some. It's in the kitchen."

"You're not eating?"

"Not for awhile yet."

Bailey fixed a large bowl, grabbing a pack of crackers on his way to the back porch. As he took his first bite, he found his mind drifting to Jonathan. It wasn't like the boy to take much interest in what Bailey said. Jonathan was never rude, but was always looking for a way to escape the conversation.

He remembered when he told Arielle the story of his paintings. The girl's face had brightened and the two had sat for hours going through the tale. Arielle was the kind that didn't care how old you were or where you were from. Her interest in his stories had been genuine, and she seemed to understand how much sharing them meant to him. Most of the folks he knew, both old and young, were like Jonathan. Bored to tears when the old man started talking, dismissing him as quickly as they could for whatever reason.

"Well I gotta get going Bailey; I need to do such and such."

"Wish I could stay longer but I have to pick up so and so."

He supposed most were like that. Being young meant things to do and people to see. The world was running by and heaven forbid they stop long enough to notice something.

Bailey could remember a time when he himself shrugged off the old men who'd talk for hours about the old days. Places long dead and people he would never meet. Now he was the old man and he tried to keep his talking in check. It was hard to do sometimes, especially days when Abbey was bad and the only company he had was himself. He wasn't one to complain much, most times he was fine keeping his own company, but sometimes the sound of someone else's voice made him feel less forgotten.

The stew was nearly gone. It had been a good batch. When her mind was clear, Abbey could cook a meal as good as anyone. He'd tell Jonathan about his painting if the boy was really interested in hearing. The story was a long one, but one he didn't tell often. In any case, he'd make it a point to go over the next morning.

He gathered up his bowl and made his way back inside. He washed his own dish, he didn't believe in all that "woman's place" nonsense, and went into the den to sit with Abbey. She was still knitting, but the look of confusion on her face was disheartening.

"I meant to ask you, Bailey, have you seen my purple shawl? I had it out for dinner last night but I can't remember where I left it."

"No, but I'll keep an eye out for it."

"I wish you would, it's worrying me."

To the untrained ear the question was a legitimate one. To Bailey, it was just the disease getting worse. He bent over and kissed her forehead.

"I'm going up to bed."

She smiled over the glasses sitting low on her nose. "See you in the morning."

Abigail would fall asleep in the chair she was in. He would find her there in the morning, her glasses crooked, her knitting askew. Looking at her like that made him feel more alone than ever. The girl he'd known was beginning to fade. The body she housed was for all intents and purposes still hers. The things that lay within her mind though were not permanent. That was what confused him the most. He did believe in God, in some form or another, but he wondered if the removal of the mind was a trick of the devil. If those thoughts left, where did they go and once they were gone would they ever come back?

The fact that an idea could be housed within an organism made of matter was strange enough to him, the spirituality of a soul must play some part. And yet, as the fading of his sister worsened he wondered more and more about the retainment of the self and at what point the part of you that defines you disappeared into the dark.

He got the blanket from the sofa and put it over

her. She snuggled in to it as she'd always done, unconscious and yet still there, and went back to sleep without ever fully coming awake.

Jonathan was watching television when the knocking began. When no one elected to get it, he strode through the living room to the door. Mr. Hazelwood was standing on the porch, white hair combed but trying to blow around.

"Good morning." Bailey said smiling.

"Hey."

"We got interrupted yesterday; I thought you might like to hear the rest of my story."

Jonathan felt an uneasy sensation drop over him. If he started listening to Mr. Hazelwood's stories, the man might always be trying to tell him one. "I don't know." He started, then saw the man's smile falter a little. There was a hugeness to the gesture and it stirred something in his head. For a moment the world got swimmy and he had to blink away the strange patterns forming around the man.

"Could you hold on just a second?"

"Sure." It was just as well. Bailey had expected the boy might not want him hanging around.

Jonathan shut the door and shook off the feeling. When his head cleared he went into the living room.

Bailey assumed he would return with the excuse, "Mom says I can't go right now," or something to that effect. What did return was the yelling of goodbye, and the reopening of the door. Jonathan came through wearing a different shirt. The boy pulled the big door shut and stepped out of the screen one.

"You mind if we go somewhere else? Mom likes to eavesdrop on me."

Bailey smiled. "Sure."

The two headed down the street away from their homes. As they went, Bailey began to speak and didn't stop until well into afternoon.

# Chapter Five

Dark skin loomed above him. The tanned chest of his brother Abraham clouded the world from his vision. It was eleven o'clock, but already the sun was scorching. California in the late thirties wasn't exactly paradise. The land was dying wherever you went. Bailey lay in the remnants of a hay pile watching clouds drift past. When the ominous figure of his older brother shrouded him in darkness, he started.

"What are you doing out here? You know pa needs you up at the house."

"I was just taking a break. The grounds a lot harder out here."

"I think maybe you're a lot softer."

Anger touched his face. "I ain't neither."

Abraham extended his hand. Bailey took it. "Go on 'n get up there."

The younger brother stood. Abraham was a good foot taller than him, with arms hardened from years of work. Most of the older men were much thinner, his father included. Even Bailey was smaller than he'd like to be. The simple fact was there wasn't enough food.

Bailey stood and brushed himself off. Abraham replaced the hat he wore to its sun blocking location and turned back towards the little acreage of field that wasn't hopeless. Bailey headed back in the direction of the house. It would take a good ten minutes to get there. He continued to watch the clouds as he went, the real reason he'd come out in the first place. His mother had made him a new shade of paint and he thought the clouds might be a good subject. Settling his sights on the ones looming above their home, he began to walk.

The house had been built by his grandfather and would be long destroyed by the time Bailey left California. He could see the outline of his father throwing feed into their truck. They'd come up with a bit extra that month and their neighbors, the Claiborne's, had asked to trade for some supplies.

"Where you been boy? I'm almost done."

"I was out in the field having a look around."

His father picked up another bag and threw it into the truck. "Field's been there since you were born son, don't think there's no need to go looking around it when we got work to do."

"Yes sir."

"Go bring that other bag down here; we gotta be out by noon."

Bailey went to the barn and began lugging the bag back up the trail. He was covered in dust from head to foot. It had been a long spell since the rain came through.

"Get on up in the back with it, we need to get on the road."

Bailey pulled the bag up and sat down on top of the other two. His father started the engine.

The ride to the Claiborne's house gave Bailey the opportunity to resume his cloud watching. Hands behind his head, he plucked a piece of straw from the truck bed and lay back. It was a rare thing to see clouds on the horizon. Even his normally stoic sister had commented on them. Bailey didn't think they would drop any rain, but they were nice to look at just the same. The tops were crested white against the hard blue of mid afternoon. White paint was easy to come by and he thought he could capture their texture without much trouble. He wished they'd been closer to the gray his mother had prepared, but his mind could imagine them soaked full of rain, darker than the shadows they cast perhaps.

That was the only thing on his mind when the truck began to slow. Knowing they hadn't gone far enough to be at the Claiborne's, Bailey sat up. Ahead was another truck with a man in overalls squatting beside the front tire. One of the wheels had gotten caught in the ruts along the road.

"Offer you some help there?" Bailey's father called.

"Got her stuck looks like."

Bailey's father stopped the truck. "Let's have a look."

The two men stood looking at the tire, swapping ideas on how to set it free. In the front seat Bailey could see the outline of a woman. In her arms was a little girl. He let his eyes drift back to the items loaded in the back and he saw two more children jump out from behind them. One was a boy closer to Abbey's age than his. The other was a blonde girl who looked to be his age. The two went around to their mother's side of the truck and began talking with her. Bailey couldn't hear what they were saying but they didn't sound too happy about whatever it was.

"I think if we give it a pull back, you can turn it left and roll across the top of it."

The man who owned the truck thought it over and agreed.

Bailey stayed in the back while the two men wrestled the truck free. They stood breathing heavily, sweat glistening on their foreheads.

"I appreciate the help."

"It's no problem, where you heading?"

"We're looking for work."

"What kind of experience you got?"

"Mostly corn and peas, potatoes, I can run a plow as good as the next un."

# KINGDOM

It was a lucky break. They'd been coming up on harvest time and his father needed more help than he had.

"Tell you what; I got a patch of land down the road a ways. We don't need plowing just now, but we do have a few acres of harvesting to do. I can't offer you much; a percentage of what you help do is about all."

"We'd be happy to take it."

"My name's Frank Hazelwood. We've got to run some feed down to our neighbor's. If you'll wait here, you can follow us back."

Bailey saw the men shake hands.

The days of the harvest came as summer slipped out. It had been late August when they'd run across the Claiborne family. Since then, Bailey had taken a liking to the blonde girl, Camille. They'd talk on the porch sometimes or in passing and he began to harbor a secret crush on her. He didn't know it then, but she felt the same way towards him. It was the crush that would set into motion the best and last of his paintings.

It was dusk. The sky blazed with orange light. He and Camille sat on the front steps of the main house talking. Her face was smeared with dirt from a day of playing in the fields. Her blonde hair clung to her face in darkened strands. Bailey found the contrast of the light against her skin mesmerizing.

"What you looking at me for?" There wasn't a hint of anger, only questioning.

"No reason."

"Well then why you still doing it?"

Bailey averted his gaze. "So you and your family are leaving come winter?"

"Yeah, pa said we'd be heading out round this time next week."

"Where you headin?"

"Don't know really. We always find somewhere."

"You like moving around?"

Camille frowned. "No, I'm always leaving something behind."

"Like your hat or something?"

"No, like people I feel for." She looked at him then and he felt a warm in his belly.

"Well, pa says the world is how it is, ain't no changing it."

"I suppose." She leaned back against the porch rail, the shadows accenting her face.

"I want to give you something." Bailey heard himself blurt.

Camille didn't look at him. "Okay. Where you want to give it to me?"

It dawned on him that she'd misread his meaning and at the same time offered him something herself. Bailey stood and took her hand. The two walked down the dirt path away from the house.

Talking was near minimum. The two relished the feeling of the others hand, the way the earth was going dark, the sweet smell of hay. When they'd gone far enough and couldn't see the house, Camille stopped under a grove of trees. Before Bailey knew what was happening, she rose on her toes and kissed him. The texture of her lips sent shockwaves through his body. He felt himself kissing her back and the sensation coated his mind.

When she pulled back, their eyes were swimming. The lines of her face against the background of sky felt as close to perfection as he'd ever come. In the grove a timid wind rolled through sending the leaves into song. As the pitch fell, the crickets became audible to his ears.

"I think I love you." He said, his voice a wavering pitch he didn't recognize.

"I think I love you too."

It was the restless world perhaps, the fact that they didn't have much longer with each other. In a world of childhood, the adults owned the sails. Each ship was a random crossing, each ocean an eternity.

"I might never see you again."

"I know."

They sat down in the grass, her head on his chest. "I can make it better." She said, her voice so low he could scarcely hear her.

He ran his fingers across her forehead, brushing away the hair which lay there. "How?"

What she said next startled him. It wasn't that it was an odd question, it was just he didn't think anyone but his mother knew.

"You paint don't you?"

Bailey didn't answer for a moment. "Been known to."

"Are you good?"

"Better 'an some, worse than others I suppose."

"I can make it better." She repeated nuzzling her head against his chest.

"How?"

"My mama comes from old blood. Way back from places I ain't ever gonna see. Mama's a painter, did you know that?"

How could he? "No."

"I want you to paint me a picture."

"I can do that."

"But it has to be what I want, and exactly how I want it. No addin in your own."

"Whatever you want, I'll put it down."

"Meet me back here tomorrow night. Bring your paint with you, all the colors you can find."

"How'm I gonna paint in the dark?"

"You're not, I'm gonna tell you bout what I want, and you're gonna get it straight in your head."

"What do I need the paint for?"

"I need to see what kind you got so I'll know what you can or can't do, kinda hard to paint a tree without any green."

"I got green."

"You catch my meaning."

He did.

She pulled herself to his mouth and kissed him again. He was instantly back in a world where nothing was wrong, everyone was good, and nothing else mattered but her.

Lying in bed that night he found himself preparing for his masterpiece. He would make whatever she wanted into the grandest painting she'd ever seen and with that he'd better his place in her memories. He'd always thought there was nothing worse than being forgotten.

The following day rolled by. He'd seen Camille only once, the dirty white of her dress flapping restless in the wind. She held one hand to her forehead, blocking the sun. It pained him to know she'd be leaving. The urgency of night seemed to slow the day to an almost unbearable pace. When the sun finally began to sink behind the trees, he burned with anticipation.

It was dusk as he slipped out of the house, an armful of paints perched in his arms. He'd brought three colors, blue, red and green, and two pigments of white and black. He could make any color with the combinations and he hoped Camille would approve. She sat on the porch, leaning back on her arms looking out across the night.

"You ready?" She asked.

"I am if you are."

With that said she stood, saw the paints in his arms, and smiled. "Let me help."

She plucked the red and green from his left hand and started walking. Bailey fell in beside her.

"You figure out what you want yet?"

"Yeah."

Bailey waited for her to elaborate, she didn't.

They walked awhile without speaking, the sounds of their feet on packed dirt echoing in the dark. Camille stepped into the grove of trees and Bailey followed, pushing back low hanging branches. Camille made her way to a clearing and sat down, patting the ground next to her. Bailey sat, feeling a stir as their arms touched.

"I'm gonna need you to do what I ask now."

"Okay."

"Close your eyes."

Bailey did, expecting another round of kisses, but none came. What did come was rustling as the remainder of the paint was taken from him, followed by a lid being loosened.

Camille set the lid aside, checking to see if Bailey's eyes were still closed. She dipped two fingers into the jar and came out with a powder that she let drift into the paint. There was a small stick beside her and she picked it up, stirring the mix. The rapid spinning made clinking sounds. Bailey turned but kept his eyes closed.

Satisfied with the consistency, she repeated the process, pausing only to get a new stick to keep the colors fresh. When finished, she brought out a pack of matches and lit the makeshift spoons. They sparked up.

Bailey could smell the familiar scent of paint mingled with smoke. Camille watched the sticks burn, her face an orange glow.

"Can I open yet?"

Her eyes never left the flame. "No."

Bailey could see light against the outside of his eyes but didn't dare open them. When the sticks were burned to Camille's satisfaction, she scooped the black husks and placed them in another jar. She replaced the top and put them back into her pocket.

"Open up."

Bailey did. The fire was gone and all his paints were lined up in front of Camille. "So what's the secret?"

"No secret, just needed to do something. I'm ready to tell you what I want, you ready?"

Bailey nodded.

Camille went into her other pocket and brought out a picture. Bailey couldn't tell what it was, but could make out there were two people in it. Camille scooted next to him and held the picture up. "That's my cousin, Mary."

Bailey could see the resemblance, both were beautiful.

"It was just before she died."

Bailey took the picture and held it closer. "What happened to her?"

"She fell."

"Fell?"

"Off her pa's barn, she had gone up to fetch something for him and slipped coming back down."

"I'm real sorry."

"Mama said its part of life." She took the picture back and looked at him. "I want you to paint this Bailey, just like it is. Do you think you can?"

Bailey thought about it. "I can give it a try. Can't promise you'll like it though."

"I'll like it as long as you remember one thing."

"What?"

"Don't be adding your own, paint it like it is."

He took another look at the picture, it wasn't in color, but he didn't think that would matter. He could tell the season by the full trees behind the girls.

"You ain't got much time, maybe a week."

"I'll do my best to get it finished for ya."

Camille looked hard at him. "There's one more thing I want you to do."

"What?"

"Don't put me in it."

"How'm I gonna do that?"

"You ain't gonna paint over that far. Just paint here." She put her hand across the image. "That's all I want."

Bailey thought about questioning further but didn't see the need. She wanted what she wanted, and what was it to him anyway? He wanted to give her what she asked no matter how strange it seemed to him.

He placed the picture in his shirt pocket and Camille took his hand. "Thank you."

The words were followed by a kiss which filled his mind with sweet honey.

They returned to the farm late in the evening. The moon was beginning to crest the sky, heading back down into the west. In his room, Bailey continued to look at the picture. It wasn't to study it, simply to see her face again, the girl with the light eyes and cropped blonde hair. In the picture the eyes were colorless, but the face was her face. The face he conjured whenever the day went too slow, the face that took him away from the heat of afternoon and into the tranquility of his heart.

The picture was begun the following night after all the lights were extinguished. The paper he selected was from his best stock, the one that hadn't been wrinkled, soaked, or stepped on. He began with Mary, tracing the outlines of her crossed hands, the contrast of her dress as it ran along her shoulders, and the smile which hung so effortlessly on her face. He continued to work until the first light of morning shone through his window.

It would take him four days to finish. Each night he got less sleep, as the picture continued to reveal itself. By the forth night it was finished, save for a few small details. Camille hadn't asked about it yet, but he caught questioning glances anytime they passed by one another. He'd give a smile to let her know it was coming along.

On the afternoon of her second to last day he gave her a nod. She took his meaning and the smile he'd been staring at alone in his room broke across her face. As the last full day came, they promised to meet in the grove after sunset. Bailey retreated to his room to give the picture one final look, making sure everything was how she wanted it. There was no need to change anything; he'd done a good job.

When he arrived at the grove, picture tucked neatly under his arm, she was already there. The wistful expression of her face was a shadowed ember in the dark night. He'd brought a small candle from the kitchen in the event they'd need light. He took it out and twisted it into the dirt until it stood firm and touched a match to it. The small circle of light brought the surrounding world to life. Camille's gaze passed from his eyes to the parchment. He was terrified once he unrolled it that it wouldn't be good enough.

Her hand brushed against his as she took it from him. She unrolled it, careful not to crease or bend it. As the image came into view an expression of shock spread across her face, followed by awe, then a look of happiness so pure he relaxed a little.

"Did I do a good job?"

For a moment she didn't speak, couldn't speak. "It's beautiful, Bailey. Perfect."

She ran her hand down the paper, feeling the lines of paint beneath it. Then she whispered a word so inaudible Bailey almost didn't hear. "Mary."

The two sat silent bathed in candlelight. The next day she would be gone, walking out of his life and into one he'd never cross into again.

When Camille finally spoke it startled him. "I want you to promise me something."

Bailey met her eyes. "Anything."

"If anything happens tomorrow, anything that you might think strange, don't tell no one about our time out here. Don't tell no one about this painting."

"I won't, you expecting some kind of trouble?"

"I hope not."

As was her way, she didn't elaborate. Bailey didn't want to push with her. He was happy sitting in the dark with her next to him. He would have kept on sitting but Camille stood up.

"I gotta get back to the house, there's some errands I got to take care of."

"This late?"

"Only time I can. I want to thank you for my picture, it's very beautiful."

"I'm glad you liked it."

"Remember, don't say nothin to nobody."

"I won't."

Back in his bed, the lack of sleep he'd been skipping caught back up with him. He was asleep as soon as his head hit the pillow.

The sound of a slamming door woke him. A beam of dust floated from the window to the floor in an exquisite array of drifting. Someone was running down the porch outside. He saw a shape go past his window. Sitting up, a small fold of paper fell from his chest. It drifted into the blazing dust beam, blinding him as it crossed through.

"Ain't over here." He heard someone shouting.

Bailey threw his legs out of bed and sat down on the floor. He scooped up the paper and quickly unfolded it. There were a few scrawled sentences written upon it.

"Not your fault. I'll be fine. Remember your promise."

Footsteps approaching. He wadded the note and stuffed it under the bed. His father burst in. "Have you seen Camille?"

Bailey tried to sound calm. "No sir. Is there something wrong?"

"She's gone Bailey, all of her things are here but she's gone. Don't know if she's run off or been stole. Get up now son, help us look."

Bailey got dressed as quick as he could. What he came upon outside was chaos. Camille's mother was clutching her younger daughter screaming at her husband she knew where she went, gone down to the retrato maldecido. Cruzado en la eternidad! Bailey was thunderstruck. He could hear his father asking what she was saying, heard Camille's father saying, "it's nonsense," then heard her mother speak the same words again. This time with calm, unfaltering gaze.

"Retrato maldecido. Cruzado en la eternidad!"

"What is she saying?" Bailey's father asked the man standing beside him.

"She says, it's the cursed painting. She's crossed into eternity."

Bailey's heart dropped. The words resonated through his head. Where was that particular painting? He turned and headed back into the house. The room where Camille slept was untouched. A quick search revealed nothing. Back outside he found the scene hadn't improved.

"I'm gonna go check the grove." Bailey shouted. No one seemed to hear him. He tore off in that direction paying no heed to the shouts behind him. As he came into the clearing he saw the candle he'd left. It had been reduced to a pool of wax. There were strange footprints in the dirt, most made when they'd been there together but there was a new set now, bare feet.

These circled the candle in random loops before moving west into the trees. Bailey didn't have to go far to see where they stopped. Laying face down in a small patch of weeds, some three hundred feet from the candle was the picture. Bailey picked it up, turned it around and found he couldn't breath.

It was the picture he'd drawn, no doubt. Yet it wasn't the same. In the place where Mary had been there were now two girls. The first thought that came was insane yet so sure.

She'd gone in.

The entire world slowed. Next to the place he'd picked up the painting, something glittered in the growing light. Bailey went to it, pushing aside the weeds. There were two glass jars. One was filled with powder; the other burned wood. As he picked up the last one, a note drifted from the bottom. He sat down in the grass and picked it up.

"I didn't tell you, you wouldn't have believed it anyway. You might have tried to stop me, and that would be worse. I'm so tired of moving around. Ma and Pa both won't say if it'll ever change. Times are tough and it's the way the world is. Well I'm tired of this world. I'm going to find Mary. I trust you to burn this. Mama will already know what I've done, pa will too. Don't worry bout trying to explain, just let it be. Thank you for the picture, if it's still here then it was better than I could have hoped. Keep it if you want to and don't feel guilty. It's not your fault. The powder I left for you. Use it for yourself if you ever get lost. Thank you for everything, Camille."

Bailey continued to look at the note, the words running together. He couldn't get his mind around what she was suggesting. Fearing his own punishment, he put the note in his pocket and gathered the rest of his things. He ran home, taking the long way so he wouldn't be seen. There were groups of men, no longer just his father and Camille's, some of the men wore uniforms going in and out of the barn, through the field, into the house. He waited until a group of three came out before slipping into the kitchen door.

He scooped a handful of matches from the stove and almost screamed as a man he didn't recognize came tearing through.

"Boy, have you seen a girl come through here? Blonde, about this high?" He made a gesture that was too tall for Camille and Bailey shook his head, trying not to look as terrified as he felt. The man heard something outside that caught his attention and tore back out of the kitchen.

Bailey watched him leap off the porch and run towards the barn. Bailey turned without another thought and headed out the rear of the house. It was covered from view and he stayed out of site until he was deep in the fields. Once the voices were too low to hear, he took out the note and touched a match to it. He waited for it to burn, careful not to set the dry grass aflame. Her words curled and died in his fingers. Once it was ash he covered it with dirt and sat there staring into the sky. What had he just been party too? What had he done?

The shouting continued until the voices were hoarse and the day was near done. Night came and the authorities left.

At dinner no one spoke. Camille's mother refused

to talk to anyone and continued to glare at Bailey until the room was empty and everyone had gone to bed. She caught him alone in the hallway and assured him in broken English that she knew where her daughter had gone, that what he had done was no laughing matter.

"There are dangerous things child, that she is not prepared for. You are too young to know what you have done. You have delivered her into Hell."

It was all it took. Hours of worry and the knowledge of what he'd done spilled forth. "I did what she asked me to, she was tired of moving around!"

"Ha! That stupid girl has no idea how much moving she'll be doing now. They will never stop chasing her, don't you see?"

"They won't find her. She ain't here no more."

"They ain't the ones I'm talkin' about." She said, mocking his accent. "They gonna find her in the dark and tear her eyes out."

She lunged at him then, grabbing his arm and squeezing so tight he screamed. He pushed her and managed to pull away long enough to get to his room and slam the door. She continued to scream at him through it as he hid the jars. If the old woman found him with them he might be arrested, or worse, they might try to take them away. He lay awake all night listening to the wails of Camille's mother. After seeing the crazed look in the old woman's eyes he wasn't sad he'd helped Camille. Wherever she'd gone, it had to be better than here.

The weeks wound out and when no sign of Camille

was found her parents eventually moved on. The jars were kept safe and the painting out of site. As months turned to years, he felt the strange confusion in him fade and the guilt he associated with it followed.

# Chapter Six

"That ain't true." Jonathan said

Bailey chuckled. "Every word."

Jonathan looked for jest in the man's face and found none.

"You still got the jars?"

Bailey knew the question well; he'd heard it after every telling. Most times he lied, said he didn't know where they were, but maybe this time he'd tell the truth, he did that from time to time. "Why do you want to know?"

"Just curious."

Bailey paused for effect, looking up into the sky

as if something there held his attention. "Might be they're still around somewhere, but I'm an old man, memories going."

Jonathan could see he was being teased. "Yeah, I bet."

Bailey laughed.

"You ever use em?"

The laughter stopped. "It's getting late; we'd probably better get back."

Jonathan tried to push but the topic was closed.

The two walked the short distance home in silence. Jonathan was intrigued at the prospect of magic powder, Bailey was shaken.

He watched Jonathan climb the steps and wave before disappearing inside. Bailey could see the light on at his own house; Abbey was in the kitchen. The old man stood watching the leaves slide across Baker Street. The smell of earth was heavy. In his mind's eye he saw Camille spinning in circles down the sidewalk, her hair a cylinder of gold. In the flash of a passing headlight, he saw her turn to him. Then she was gone.

Inside he found Abbey in the kitchen. She looked up from her writing and smiled. "Did he like your story?"

"Seemed to."

"Yeah, I know I liked to hear it but I suppose I'm biased. Are you hungry?"

"No. I was thinking I'd turn in early."

Abbey knew telling the story always changed Bailey's mood. It was worse when they were younger, when the teasing was apt to follow. "I'll leave some meat out, in case you get hungry."

Bailey turned in but sleep eluded him. Why did he have to remember it? It wasn't enough that he thought the whole thing was his fault. What had he done really that was so bad? Camille wanted to go, she just didn't have the talent to do it. Bailey had freed her. What difference did it make what her parents thought? What mattered was Camille. It was the only train of thought he allowed himself to hold, the only thing that allowed him justify what he had done. Yet had it worked? Here he sat, just like the boy he was, remembering.

In another house on the same street, Jonathan was also sitting alone. Sleep had come easy but so had the dreams. These latter pulled him from the previous with enough venom to keep him up. They were dreams of Arielle, swirling concoctions of his mind's mania. They pulsed through his blood, widening his eyes and quickening his heart. It didn't matter that he couldn't go back to sleep, didn't matter that the things he saw weren't real. What did matter is how he felt about the story. What if it had been true?

The following morning while waiting for the school bus, Jonathan spied the old man looking down from an upstairs window. Jonathan threw him a wave and Bailey returned it. He could hear the building groan of the bus in the distance. When it arrived, he climbed on and took a seat near the back. His house was closer to the beginning of the route and the bus wasn't full yet. He scooted over to the window.

The world began to move as the breaks released.

## JEREMY RANDOLPH

If nothing else, the jars took his mind off Arielle. The prospect of a new mystery was one she'd have appreciated. Perhaps she'd even investigated herself. He made a promise to himself to find out. If they did exist, then he would see them. He doubted if Mr. Hazelwood would allow him to use them, but what if he did? The prospect made him giddy.

The daydreaming continued through his first two periods. There were so many questions he wanted to ask, so many things to further his fascination. He wanted to run home and hound Mr. Hazelwood until the man told him everything, every minute detail, but he wasn't sure if it was such a good idea. What if the jars were gone? Jonathan enjoyed the feeling of having something he could get his mind on, something to occupy it during the empty spaces.

By lunchtime he was void of any other thought. The day was crawling. Every few minutes he'd steal a glance at the clock on the cafeteria wall and swear it wasn't moving.

"Whatcha late for?" Charlotte Holt, a girl from his homeroom, had noticed him looking up and decided to get involved. She was overweight and prone to irritation. Her brown hair fell in curls around her oversized head.

"Nothing." Jonathan said and started eating hoping to end it.

"Must be late for something, you look at that clock again you're gonna get whiplash."

"Yeah, old Johnny here's late for a date." It was Russell Harris. Russell was the type of kid who knocked your books out of your hands and tried to play it off as you picked them up. Jonathan loathed people who hid meanness behind humor. Comments like, "I was just kidding, " or "Dang, take a joke."

Jonathan didn't reply and hoped the boy would leave it. He didn't. "Who's the lucky lady? Mrs. Pines?"

This drew a wave of laughter from the table.

"Yup, that's the one. She's gonna meet you out behind the gym, stick her tongue in your mouth."

Charlotte made a disgusted face and went back to eating her potatoes.

"She gonna have your baby?"

Jonathan hadn't seen who made the comment but he could feel his jubilation fading to anger. Arielle had told him to ignore them, it wasn't the first time they'd come at him like this. He wasn't the only butt of the groups joke, but he was one of Russell's favorite. He'd broken all the other kids, made them cry or yell. It was probably the reason he was still after Jonathan, the boy refused to crack.

"I bet her husband would be real happy to hear you're banging her." Another caw of laughter.

Jonathan had managed to steer clear of Russell the past few months, change paths on the way to class, avoid certain bathrooms, even going so far as to show up late to class, today however he'd been thinking of Bailey and the jars and hadn't noticed when the boy sat down at his table. Now he was under full cafeteria assault.

"Why don't we go over there after school and let

him know?" The comment got the loudest laughter yet.

Jonathan checked the clock. Fifteen more minutes.

"What's wrong lover boy? Am I making you mad?"

Jonathan looked into the boy's eyes. A funny thing had happened since Arielle left. Before, Jonathan would feel anger but would always control himself. Now, there was a vacancy in the place which held him back. The doorman had stepped aside, leaving the floodgates unmanned.

"You're just a little pussy." Russell said. "At least your parents still have one daughter left."

Jonathan felt the sensation of restraint snap. It broke in his mind like a tree in a hurricane and the emotion poured forth, taking with it any chance he had of control.

Charlotte, the girl who'd inadvertently started the whole thing, was raising her fork to her mouth. There was a large portion of potatoes hanging on the end of it and before she could react Jonathan had torn it from her hand. The potatoes she'd been so looking forward to eating flew from their perch and landed in a wad on the front of her shirt. She started to protest but Jonathan pushed her back and threw himself across the table. Russell, who'd turned to watch the kid beside him laugh, didn't see the flash of metal as it crossed towards him. Jonathan snatched the front of the boy's shirt and twisted it. The forward motion sent both of them backwards. Russell hit the floor hard and screamed. Jonathan landed on top of him and brought the fork hard into the tender skin beneath his chin stopping just before it broke through.

Russell's eyes were terrified. Jonathan could hear the approaching hoards of teachers and pushed the fork harder. Four small pinpoints of blood appeared beneath it. The kids who'd been laughing so hard earlier backed even further away. Some of them ran for cover, not caring how the act before them played out.

"Talk about her again, I dare you."

Jonathan felt the first hands against his back. They tried to pull him up but he wouldn't come. An arm went around him and as it pulled him backward, Jonathan spit into Russell's face. The fork fell onto the floor and slid beneath the table.

The rumors swirled for months about what had happened. Everybody had their own version, but in almost all Jonathan was made out to be a crazy person. Both boys were suspended and in an odd touch of irony Russell received five days to Jonathan's three. Everyone knew Jonathan was a good kid, a boy who'd lost a sister. Russell was a constant nuisance to both the students and the staff. Some of the teachers silently rejoiced in the incident wishing that Jonathan would have done more to the boy than just scare him. None of the teachers had seen the fork in his hand, and if some did, they didn't say anything about it. Russell refused to say anything about anything, especially with Jonathan in the room, he was too afraid. There was a series of small holes under his chin but there was also a grove of pimples and they drew no attention.

Russell never spoke to Jonathan again. He made

a point to steer clear of him whenever he saw him in the halls. The eyes that had looked down at him in the cafeteria had been so void of consequence that he sometimes had nightmares about them. Jonathan was banned from leaving the house for two weeks. Both parents understood why he'd attacked, but couldn't condone it for any reason.

Jonathan spent most of his grounded days staring out his bedroom window watching the movement of the world and being content on his absence from it. On many occasions he saw Mr. Hazelwood pass on his afternoon walks. The old man never turned towards the house, nor did he look up at Jonathan's window and Jonathan began to wonder if it was intentional.

At night he'd sneak to the churchyard and sit high above the town. He'd talk to Arielle, relating the events of his day and hoping for some message or sign. None came. Most times he found himself remembering what it felt like to be up here knowing she was at home in bed, sleeping as the rest of the world slept. Now she slept below him, six feet under the ground. He stared down trying to find her grave and once again found the strange need to draw consume him. As it always was, the subject was an unexpected one, moving as it would along its own path.

Brady Coleman was a name the local children would invoke when the subject of serial killers or madmen came up. The tales were always broad with facts no one could dispute or disprove. Some claimed he was an escaped rapist from Georgia. Others claimed he was a bank robber from Tennessee. The most undisputed claim was that he had murdered a family on Christmas Eve.

Now the man, who'd come to Morning Ridge to take care of his ailing mother, walked with a limp towards the small bench on the southwest side of the cemetery. He was wearing a pair of dirty green coveralls with something square in his back pocket. Jonathan felt a small twang of fear but held steady. Brady took his seat on the bench and unzipped the front of his suit. He took a rag from his pocket and proceeded to wipe the sweat from his brow.

He'd been out digging for a funeral. Unknown to Jonathan, the man felt it best to get the work done before the family arrived. There was something primitive about digging a hole in the earth to place a body in. Most didn't like that reality staring back at them. Seeing the earth moving, the weight of it, the way it spilled off the digger, that was enough to send even the strongest man into thoughts of mortality.

Jonathan could see Brady had a book in his back pocket. The man took a flashlight from his other pocket and placed it on his shoulder and began leafing through the pages. It was an unexpected scene and something in it brought the winding up sensation Jonathan had felt with the snowball girl. A sudden rise of laughter pulled his eyes away and the world exploded with light. The scene froze in his eye, ripping through his mind. There was a strange ringing in his ears and he fancied the world was still glowing around the edges. Shaken, he climbed down. Brady, engulfed in reading, never looked up.

Once home he went to his room. With shaking hands he took the wooden box from the closet. With long strokes he began to purge himself of the whatever it was that held him. Before his eyes, he watched it unfold. The deep edges of Brady's face were enhanced giving the man a haunted look. The hands did their work as they would, much too easy for a boy with no training.

It took almost six hours before the final pass of his finger. When it was done, the odd sensation of urgency left him and he felt purged of the need. Lifting the finished product to the moonlight, he witnessed the long creased face of Brady Coleman; saw the man reading the worn pages of his paperback and behind him hundreds of restless spirits wound their way into the night sky.

# Chapter Seven

Jonathan managed to hold off questioning Bailey for three months. It was hard to do, but he feared the loss of his new mystery. Once the story was told, there would be nothing left but the truth and if the truth turned out to be less than he'd built in his mind, the familiar emptiness would creep back in. He picked up the phone on a Saturday. He wanted to call first, so he could gauge Bailey's mood and leave both of them with an escape if the conversation went bad. He needed to be careful how and what he asked. He dialed the numbers and waited.

Next door Bailey heard the onset of the telephone

but didn't move for it. His back was hurting and he didn't feel much like walking around. After two more rings it became apparent Abbey wasn't going to pick it up so he stood and made his way across the room.

"Hello?" He hoped like hell it wasn't a salesman, be damned those people always calling him.

"Mr. Hazelwood?"

A young voice, one he recognized, "yes?"

"Hey, it's Jonathan."

"Yes, Jonathan, how are you?"

"I'm okay. Listen, I wanted to ask, and if you say no it's fine, really, but do you think we could meet at the church and talk some more?"

"Is something wrong?"

"No, I just needed to ask you something."

"Well I suppose I could do for a walk, what time?"

"Whenever you get out there is fine."

"Well, give me about twenty minutes to get up and moving."

The two met on the church steps with Bailey looking frail and Jonathan bundled in a green coat. Jonathan sat on the top step, Bailey one below it leaning back on his arm. It was a hazy afternoon and the sun was lost behind a hue of clouds. It had been almost a year since Arielle, and Jonathan found no solace in the passing of time.

Bailey understood what the boy wanted. Even before he'd gotten the call to come meet him he knew. It was inevitable that the question would need to be answered, and it might be a good thing to get it out of the way as soon as possible. The boy didn't know it, but Bailey was under the weather more than he'd like lately. It was part of the reason he stayed away from the boy. He didn't want him getting too attached to an old man, especially one who couldn't get rid of his new cough. But, he'd agreed to come, not knowing how he would handle it.

The boy was already waiting when he arrived. The two sat in silence. It wasn't an uncomfortable silence but a reflective one.

"Thanks for coming out."

"No problem, though I must admit, your choice of venue is quite unusual."

Jonathan didn't reply at first. He knew full well why he'd chosen this place. "I wanted her to be able to hear."

Bailey took his meaning and nodded. "Good enough."

Jonathan looked down at his hands not knowing how to begin.

"I know why you wanted to talk to me."

Jonathan was startled but not surprised.

"There are some things you have to understand first. The main one might not sit well with you."

Jonathan shuffled his feet.

"I'm sure you've noticed, but I've been sick for awhile now. Doctor says I'm over it, but I don't feel over it. In any case, I'm not real sure if I'm sick or just getting old. It's probably a combination of both. I wanted to get that out of the way. You're a smart boy and you know what I'm saying."

Jonathan continued to look at his hands but nodded understanding.

"When I was your age, things were different, the world was different. We worked hard and did the best we could. Even in times like those, what some consider simpler times, the use of those jars was dangerous. Even when I'd lost everything I loved, I still couldn't justify using them. You don't understand how they take you in. They're not something to be taken lightly and they're certainly not something you should ever try unless you truly understand the ramifications. I never learned fully what they were capable of, but I saw enough to cast me away from ever using them again. I struggled for years over what to do with them. The better part of my conscious told me I should destroy them, but every time I tried it seemed wrong."

Bailey stared across the empty pavement and was silent for a long time. "I still have them."

The world went swimmy. Jonathan felt the light, burned almost to extinction lick up once more in his soul.

"They're in a safe place. They've been there for years and I haven't touched them since."

Cars rolled past on the main street. Pairs of children passed the churchyard laughing and shouting unintelligible words. A slow moving world was spinning out beyond their words, a place where people went home to eat dinner before sitting down in front of the television to "relax". Mothers mothered and fathers fathered. The activities of work and play intertwined in their untouched illusions of existence. But in the churchyard, two generations were locked in their understanding of the true world. The one that peeled back all you thought and exposed the hardness of life beyond perception, true reality.

"I never had a son. Of my family, only Abbey is left. I could let these things die with me, probably should. But I know that I can't do that. You're too young by far for me to explain what these jars are and I know that you've brought me here in the hope that I would give them to you if I had them. I cannot. There are too many layers to be peeled back and re-added in your life. I was too young when I came into possession of them and my naivety nearly drove me mad. I'm slowing down, but I'm not down yet. I suspect I have a few more years left in me. If you want what I have, you have to make me a promise. You have to be ready in your soul."

Jonathan hung on Bailey's words.

"Go on and live your life Jonathan. Don't worry about me, the jars or anything else. Take who you are and mold him. If I ever think that you're ready, I'll come to you. Until then, don't speak of these things again, to me or to anyone."

In the silence after, nothing moved. Jonathan had brought Mr. Hazelwood hoping to get a small piece of information. What had transpired was beyond anything he could have imagined. That the jars existed was payment enough. The rest was more than he ever hoped to let himself believe. More important than that was he had a purpose. There was something to fix his mind on. The long days of empty activities had been replaced by hope, the thought that he was working towards something. An adventure Arielle would have loved to be a part of. The thought of her brought a deep feeling of loss.

"I have to get back now. Abbey is expecting me."

Jonathan watched as the man lit a cigar and stood up.

"Mr. Hazelwood!"

The man turned.

"Thank you."

Bailey nodded and raised a hand.

Jonathan would try and do what Mr. Hazelwood had asked. It was something Arielle would have wanted for him too. He'd made a promise to her also, one which he hadn't been able to keep. He thought he might have the strength to fulfill it now.

He rode home and got the box she had given him. The sun was a ball of fire as he mounted his bike and peddled off down Baker Street. When he crossed Gideon's Circle he felt calm descend. The bike passed from asphalt to grass and he hopped off, walking through the underbrush. When he saw the creek, it was hard to breath.

The water was low and he wouldn't have trouble crossing. The bike rolled across easy. It was tougher getting it up the embankment but he managed. Then he was there, staring across the field at their place. He could make out the familiar angle of the roof.

A crow sat on the corner of the small porch looking at him as he approached. When he got close, it cawed irritation and lifted into the sky. Jonathan watched it disappear over the canopy of trees.

The days since he'd been here hadn't been kind. The rest of the unbroken windows had been busted out and the interior was full of dead leaves. It would take a bit of housework to get it back to its old glory but that would come later. First he had to get inside without coming apart.

"Go on in silly, nothing's gonna get you." It was her voice again, reciting in the patient tone she used for situations he was unsure of.

Jonathan stepped onto the porch. The shadowed interior loomed beyond the doorway. He stepped inside for the first time in ages and saw her there, sitting beneath the window writing. The soft sounds of pen on paper filled his ears. Then the image faded, turned transparent, and disappeared. Had it really been so long? He breathed in loving the scent of fresh air and old wood.

"Okay Arielle, here we go." Gathering his will, Jonathan stepped through the doorway and back into his lost revelry.

# Chapter Eight

Emily Brewington knew nothing more about what she was doing than she did about boys. It was like that every day, at least for the last three. She was beginning to realize the boys made her feel funny, especially Jonathan Murray. No matter how hard she tried she couldn't stop thinking about him. Crush was too light a word for the way she felt and she'd never even spoken to him.

Her parents wouldn't let her attend public school saying the environment, "wasn't healthy for a girl her age". Emily hadn't argued. It wouldn't have made a difference.

# KINGDOM

She'd gotten off the bus three weeks before meaning to run into the house. It was a long ride from school and she'd made the mistake of having a Coke before climbing on. Coming off the bus she ran into a kid on the sidewalk. The boy steadied her, smiled, and kept going. Something in his eyes made her heart jump and she stood there watching him walk away. Her father would have thought he was scrawny, but to Emily he was just the right everything. Forgetting about her screaming bladder, she fell in behind him being sure to stay far enough back to avoid detection.

Jonathan didn't live far from her. One right, then another put him two yards back from hers. The houses behind had blocked her previous knowledge of his existence. She took it as some sign of fate that she'd seen him. Of course they'd lived on Pepper Street for three years but still. Great forces were at work.

Since convincing herself of divine intervention, she'd taken to stalking him. It sounded bad when you said it out loud, but Emily didn't think much of it. If she happened to ride her bike down a certain street, so what, if she just happened to be sitting in the yard across from his house reading when he came outside, big deal.

But it was a big deal. Every time she saw him it felt like the air wouldn't come. What made it worse was the kid didn't acknowledge her. When he came outside, he would walk with his head down or stare straight ahead. Not once did he look in her direction. Now she sat two houses down, pretending to be lost. When Jonathan came outside, she again followed. He led her into the churchyard and she fell back more, being especially careful not to be seen. She'd lost him then, coming around the side of the church only to find him gone.

It would have surprised her to know that Jonathan knew he was being followed. He hadn't disappeared either; he'd gone into his favorite tree. From that vantage he could see the specter who he'd only suspected had been following him. Though he didn't know her, he'd seen her once a few weeks before. She'd come off of a Holy Trinity school bus and nearly knocked him down. Now the girl looked confused, staring back and forth. He thought about giving up his position but didn't know her intention. Instead, he waited until she turned back for home then fell in behind her. As she stood beneath the light of her front porch, he could see familiar features on her face. Not able to place them, he watched her disappear into the warmth of the house.

Emily had no idea he was behind her. Her head was turning this way and that, wondering why in the world she was acting so crazy. She had an idea that if she ever did talk to him, her head might explode.

Her parents were in the living room and her mother asked where she'd been. Emily said walking, which was the truth. Her father asked if she'd like to watch TV with them but Emily declined. She wanted to get upstairs and get on her pj's.

In the comfort of her room, she let his face come to her. The worst of it was she didn't even know his name. She hoped it was something good.

Two yards over, Jonathan sat on the porch. The intrigue of being followed was an enigma worth dwelling on. Nothing good could come of it. When girls started following you around, it meant one of two things. They liked you or they hated you. In this case, the latter was probably true. Running into him couldn't have felt good.

Two old women passed on the sidewalk walking a small dog. Jonathan raised his hand and they waved back.

"Trying to pick up girls again, eh?"

The voice was shocking in its clarity and it was one he recognized. His father had come out onto the porch. "You know I think they're a little out of your league."

Jonathan shrugged, "can't knock me for trying."

His father laughed. "No I suppose not. You hungry?"

"Yeah."

"Good, go wash your hands, mom says dinner is served"

Emily stepped out of the bathroom in her pink pajamas The purple plastic shape of her telephone stared up at her, a lone daffodil sticker on its center. She picked up the receiver and dialed 411.

It took a few tries but she managed to get a number that matched the street the boy lived on. She wrote it on a scrap of paper and lay with the phone on her chest. The indecision was maddening. Twice she dialed the number and hung up before it could ring. What exactly did she plan on saying?

"Hello, I've been stalking you for the past few weeks. Can we talk?"

The thought of hearing his voice would ease her addiction. Then again, it could make it worse. Each thought she pursued only led in circles. Why was this so hard? It didn't matter that she could talk to just about anyone at school, girl or boy. It didn't matter that she'd never really been afraid of anything, least of all calling someone. Yet it was still there, a sharp burn in the pit of her stomach. The more numbers she dialed, the more pronounced it became. Twice she'd sat the phone back on the nightstand, only to pick it back up and look at it.

It was maddening. The clock read eight-thirty. She made a pact with herself that if she didn't call by eight-thirty-five, she would put the phone up and go to bed. It gave her some breathing time. Rushing through her head the reasons for and the reasons against came, each one as sensible as the one before. As the clock rounded eight-thirty-four, she snatched up the receiver and dialed the numbers. For a long moment nothing happened. Then...

Jonathan was scraping the last of his peas from his plate when the shrill sound of the telephone erupted behind him. His mother, already finished, was standing at the sink rinsing the dishes. She made no move to answer it.

Jonathan set his plate down. Reaching back, he scooped the receiver from the wall.

"Hello."

Silence.

# KINGDOM

"Hello?"

Still nothing.

Jonathan's father was looking at him eyebrows raised.

Jonathan shrugged and hung up.

Emily set the phone back in its birth, a smile blooming across her face. It was a good voice. It was only the second time in her life she'd heard it, and it was through a phone line, but it was still the drug she needed. She returned the phone to her nightstand and closed her eyes. Jonathan finished cleaning his plate and helped his mother finish drying.

The next day was Monday, no school and no parents. Summer vacation was the best invention since ice cream. Emily was up early. She'd decided she would have talk to the boy in person. It didn't matter what he thought, the whole situation was becoming insane.

Usually she didn't take her bike, walking suited her best, but today she would. There was no telling how fast her escape might have to be. She could say something totally stupid and have to make a break for it. The queer nervousness had already begun but she pushed it aside and headed down the street. Her speed was slow but understandable. It was the phone call all over again amplified to the fifth power.

She rounded his street and was shocked to see him coming up it on the other side. He hadn't seen her yet, but he would in seconds. There was no time to think, she had to get out of there. What had she been thinking? But it was too late.

Jonathan raised his hand in a wave. Emily only sat there. Jonathan saw this and put his head down.

"What are you doing?" A voice screamed in her head. She could feel time spinning out. "Hello!" Her voice boomed. Why had she done that? Surely he would run. Jonathan looked up at the sound; it had been faint to him but no matter. Before she could stop him, he crossed the street.

Jonathan knew the girl had come to follow him and thought it would be funny to wave. When she hadn't responded, he had a brief moment of stupidity. Then she'd yelled at him. Now he meant to speak with her, if for no other reason than to figure out what she was up to. As he approached, he was again struck by the familiarity in her face. Something else struck him too, she was very pretty. Now it was his turn to feel the butterflies.

Then he was there. Face to face with her. She'd dreamed of the moment for days and felt herself being pulled into him. For a moment, neither spoke, they just continued looking at each other. Jonathan broke the silence.

"Hello."

"Hi."

"Have you been following me?"

The question had a physical effect on her.

"I mean, I saw you the other day. I don't mean following me for real. I just mean..."

A smile came then and he relaxed a little. "I'm Jonathan."

"Emily."

"Do you go to Morning Ridge?"
"No, St. Mary's over by the bridge."
"Do you like it?"
"It's okay."
"Did you just move in?"
"Oh, no. We've been here for about three years."

Jonathan nodded. The silence threatened but he could do no more. The girl had an effect on him as well. Then an odd thing happened. The familiarity he'd been trying to place came to him. He blurted without thinking.

"Were you in a snowball fight?"

Emily was confused by the direction the conversation had taken, but she obliged. "Lots of 'em."

It dawned on him that this girl bore a striking resemblance to the blond girl he'd drawn the previous winter. The hair was the same hue of yellow, the eyes the same cool blue.

"I think I saw you once."
"You do?"
"Yeah. During a snowball fight."

Emily searched her mind but couldn't remember. "I don't know, maybe."

Sensing it was a bad direction, Jonathan tried again. "I'm gonna be going down to the church tonight. They're having some kind of dinner. Do you go to church?"

"I used to."
"Well you should come with me."

Her heart jumped again. "I'd have to ask."

"We can walk. It's not far. I think it starts at six"

"Come by my house about five then."

"Okay."

She smiled at him. "Okay."

They sat for a moment longer memorizing the faces before them. Then Emily climbed on her bike and turned for home. It was the sweetest ride she'd ever had.

At five that night he stood in front of her house. The clothes he wore were what he considered his casual church clothes. Arielle would get a kick out of him standing out here nervous, he was sure of it. With that thought the courage he needed came. He walked to the front door and rang the bell. He could hear the sounds of footsteps and the door opened. Emily stepped outside and closed it behind her.

"You ready?"

She looked at his attire. "Yeah, are these clothes okay? I forgot to ask what kind to wear."

"Yeah, you look nice."

The comment sat well with her.

"So what's this thing about?"

"It's just a dinner for the Sunday school classes. There will be some parents there, not mine, but some. Mostly kids though. It's pretty good, I went last year."

They made the walk slow, making small talk and trying not to trip or say something stupid. It was a pleasant night for walking with the moon poking through the clouds casting soft light on the sidewalk.

# KINGDOM

Jonathan prattled on like an idiot about everything from the grass to his shoes. Every now and then he'd catch himself and try to ask her a question. Emily would answer but wouldn't contribute. She liked letting him talk.

They turned off the main sidewalk to bypass the town. It would take longer, but Jonathan was enjoying the feel of night and the company he kept. Having her with him made him feel alive. They crossed through someone's yard, trying to stay out of view. On the other side, they joined the adjacent sidewalk and continued on. By the time they reached St. Andrews, they were just in time for dinner.

The church was not as full as it was on Christmas Eve, but it was busy just the same. The majority of the patrons were as Jonathan said, children. Inside a buffet table and a line of people stretched along the back wall. Steam rose from the metal containers in small puffing clouds. People piled their plates high, talking to the person behind them and looking up line to see what the holdup was. It was a festive environment and it relaxed both of them.

They took their place at the end and waited to reach the plate table. A large woman in a red dress was crowing laughter every few seconds. A man whose cheeks matched her dress kept spewing witticisms to entice this behavior. They'd scoop green beans, turn around, speak, laugh, and move on again.

It took a while to reach the food so there weren't many tables left. They managed to find a small one by the back windows. There was enough room for two more, but none took the initiative. Jonathan had assumed he'd come by himself, pretend to listen to people talking then go home. It was much better this way. Emily ate without care, dripping and talking with her mouth full.

It felt good to be with a girl who was natural. Too many of the girls at school were so concerned about looking good, they'd eat like a bird or not at all.

After dinner, they slipped out. Emily had a nine o' clock curfew and Jonathan didn't want to waste time listening to the church ladies talk coming attractions. It was a good night; the growing evening hadn't cooled the air. It was surreal to both. They went back the way they'd come, careful not to move too fast. They talked about everything and it came easy. Neither had ever been much for sharing, but now it seemed they couldn't shut up. Secrets and stories spilled from their lips as easy as water from a pipe.

Arielle would have liked Emily. The thought came to him as she was telling a story about fishing. An odd story for a girl to be telling, but that was precisely it. Emily wasn't average; she was an adventurer like him. Nothing stood in her way when it came to trying something new and when she told him of her love of drawing, it clenched the deal. By her own admission she wasn't very good, but it didn't matter. The girl was an artist.

He'd been playing with that idea since he met her. The eyes danced around things as if marking their movement. Most times he thought he was a little crazy to be making assumptions so early, but this was different. Emily spoke, thought, and even looked to him like an artist. What kind was still in debate, but enough like him to open the part of himself he kept closed from others, the people who couldn't understand his ramblings and somewhat odd behavior.

She saw the expression on his face and stopped walking. "Why are you smiling?"

Jonathan looked up. "Was I?"

"Yes."

She was trying to tell if he'd been making fun of her somehow. It wouldn't be the first time that sort of thing happened. Her aunt Elizabeth absolutely delighted in poking fun in what she'd said. That lady was a teacher and a realist of a woman. The backside of life never entered her mind. "Crazy ideas make crazy people," she was fond of saying. But no matter, the boy was the issue now.

"Are you making fun of me?"

Jonathan stiffened. "No. I was actually thinking how much I like you." Again, the words spilled out before he could tell his mouth not to say them, and what would it hurt anyway? He wasn't sure.

Emily stared at him. The look of questioning gave way to understanding, which then gave way to fascination. "I like you too. You're cooler than any of the kids I usually hang out with."

The warmth which emitted from the center of his chest was somewhat strange, somewhat wonderful. They continued on, lapsing back into the tales of their lives.

When they reached her house, the lights from

the porch still blazed. They stood for a moment in complete silence, the only one they'd shared. Jonathan heard himself start to talk about nothing, heard a strange question about the flowers beside them come out of his mouth then wondered to himself why he was so nervous.

Cool blue eyes stared back at him. They were somewhat curious but not without understanding. Emily decided to take the initiative, not sure if it was appropriate and not really caring. She went for the cheek, a neutral enough place, but felt a shiver run through her all the same. Jonathan felt it too like liquid electricity. Then she said good night, gave him a wink and opened the door.

He stood for a moment, not sure what to do next. There was no way he was going to sleep tonight. Every inch of his body was hyped up. The odd overflowing of emotion shouldn't have been surprising to him. The only emotions he'd allowed himself to feel over the past year was pain, self loathing, and sadness. Now his senses had come awake.

The walk home was the longest he'd ever had. It wasn't that the distance had changed, nor was it that he took the longest route possible. It was the fact that he stopped every second or two to look up into the sky, watch the leaves rustle, take a deep breath and remember her.

As he approached his street, he noticed a figure standing along side the gate running parallel to Bailey Hazelwood's house. A small circle of orange burned in the darkness. It was Mr. Hazelwood come outside to get some air. It had been a long night for him. The sickness in his lungs still refused to leave.

"Come on over here, boy. You got a tale to tell."

Jonathan smiled in spite of himself.

The two sat together on the edge of the street as they'd done many times before, pushing through formalities before Bailey decided to get to the heart of it.

"What's her name?"

Jonathan hadn't expected the question and looked surprised. "Who?"

"That's what I want to know. Boys your age don't glow like you are unless there's a "her" involved."

Jonathan paused. Telling Mr. Hazelwood would be okay. There was a trust between them. "Emily."

Bailey took a puff of his cigar. "Emily huh. It's a good name."

"I suppose."

"So you go to school with her?"

"No, she goes to private school."

"Rich girl, eh? Got to watch those rich girls."

"No, I don't think she's rich. They have a nice house though. She's not snooty or anything." Jonathan realized he was defending her and saw Mr. Hazelwood looking at him thoughtfully.

"I was just giving you a hard time." He began to laugh and a fit of coughing overcame him. He rocked back and forth struggling against the onset. Jonathan waited for the fit to pass, not knowing if he should try to pat his back or ignore the thing all together. After a moment, Bailey composed himself.

"Sorry about that. I can't seem to shake this cold. Sure seems to be able to shake me though, doesn't it?" He winked at Jonathan and the boy smiled. "So is she pretty?"

Jonathan felt his face flush. "Yeah, she's pretty."

Again Bailey smiled. How long ago had it been when he had felt that way? Longer than he'd cared to remember.

"So does this Emily like you back?"

Jonathan thought about it. "I don't know. I think so."

Bailey understood the uncertainty of youth's first love, second guessing was the rule of thumb.

"Well just follow your heart. Things will be as they'll be, can't change that."

Jonathan nodded. The world was still turned up a notch. "I'd better get inside, mom's gonna call the police if I'm not home soon."

"Yes, she was out on the porch awhile ago asking if I'd seen you."

Jonathan got to his feet. "Good night."

Bailey gave a wave.

Both his parents were in the kitchen playing a game of cards. They looked up when he came in, saw he wasn't bleeding from the ears, and went back to playing.

Jonathan went to his room, finding the house a bit less gloomy than it had been earlier that day. There were still a few weeks of summer vacation left. The days stretched out in a limitless bastian of possibility. He saw the two of them talking for hours, learning things about one another. It was exactly what he needed and for the first time since Arielle died, he went to sleep without giving the journal a second thought.

# Chapter Nine

Emily woke, her thoughts fixed on Jonathan. For the past seven days the two of them were inseparable. It was funny that she'd formed such a strong bond with a boy. They both knew how the other felt, but the rituals of being boyfriend girlfriend had not, of late, transpired. They would talk for hours never lacking for a topic, but the kisses she so desperately wanted had not come to pass.

At first she'd thought he wasn't interested, it was her own self doubt, but when she saw the way he looked at her she knew better. Boys talked a big game until it came down to doing, then their courage disappeared. She intended on making the first move and this time she wouldn't be aiming for his cheek.

He called that morning saying he wanted to take her somewhere. When she pressed him for more details, he wouldn't budge. So there she was, intrigued. It was what she really liked about him. No matter what they were doing, he could always keep a mystery about things, a sense of possibility in the impossible.

Jonathan had awakened with the same thoughts on his mind. It would be a beautiful day if the light streaming in his window was any indication and that would be good, because they'd need the sun. Putting on his shoes, he sent his mind out into the world. Two streets over, Emily would be waiting for him. The thought of her made the sensations of doubt fade.

It was Arielle who'd brought him to the decision he'd made the day before. Arielle whose words finally made the decision he'd been pondering a reality. It was the first time he'd opened the notebook in a long time. He wanted to see if his renewed emotions could coexist with Arielle's words. He hoped that it would give him new insight on what his life was becoming and prayed that he would find something to let him know it was okay to feel the way he did.

When he touched the cover, he felt his heart pulling him back to darkness. With a little effort he pushed it away and opened to the few remaining pages. There weren't many more of these sessions left to experience.

The soft loop of her words caught him off guard. The passage sucked him from his world back into the days when she was still there to talk and laugh with, back to the time when she was still with him.

"Moon's out tonight. Biggest one I think I've ever seen. It's hanging up there, orange as a pumpkin. Not sure how many moons I have left. Today Jonathan wanted to go to the field but I could hardly stand up. I think he could tell I wasn't feeling well cause he normally pesters me if I won't go. Today he just smiled and said okay. I don't like the way people are acting around me. The big party at Megan's is this Friday but nobody's asked me to go. None of the boys want to take the sick girl. I was hoping Eric would come around; it's been almost two weeks now since we broke up, but he hasn't. I wish I could still talk to him, it gets lonely sometimes. I try to keep my head up, dad says that's the best way to beat it, but I don't think I'm gonna win this one. The doctor told us last week the chemo isn't working. I haven't written it down until now. I think it makes it real once you write it down. I feel bad about Jonathan. I hope he doesn't stop going to our place. It'll be hard on him, but he loves it out there so much, my baby brother. I'm really going to miss him."

Jonathan's face was streaked with tears. The edge of the blade hadn't retracted as far as he'd thought. He let the burn coarse through him, all the old thoughts and memories dumping chemicals into his blood, tearing his mind apart. Once the intensity began to waver, he knew his question had been answered. If he wanted to bring Emily, Arielle wouldn't have minded. In fact, his sister would have no doubt welcomed his new friend. It was always Arielle who thought he should have more.

Now a day had passed and the sharp point of his emotions had subsided. Outside the sun spilled down warming his worn shirt. He'd picked the outfit because he knew he'd be getting dirty. The shorts he'd selected were reserved for working in the yard. They had small green stains faded into an almost indistinguishable hue. The shoes were the same with sockless feet inhabiting them. It was a summer's outfit for a summer's day.

His method of transport was a brisk walk. It was always better to walk when he was with Emily. If they rode their bikes, they couldn't talk as much and he wanted to hold on to every second with her. She was already waiting when he came up the street. The front porch was lined with yellow and blue flowers. They added enough splendor to make his heart reel again. Emily saw him approaching and smiled. She too had selected a summer's outfit per his request. The shorts and shirt were like his, worn. The only difference was her shoes. She wore a pair of purple flip-flops.

The toes which peered from these were shaped and painted. It was a painstaking ordeal she'd spent an hour on for this occasion. On her right forth toe was a small ring with a small red flower in its center. The color in it matched the color on her nails. It was an added touch she hoped he'd appreciate.

He raised his hand and she raised hers in return standing to wipe the dirt off her bottom. They met where the sidewalk touched the street.

"You ready to go?"

Emily shielded her eyes from the sun. "Yeah, but were you taking me?"

"You'll see when we get there."

They made their way back towards Jonathan's house. Emily recognized the way and thought they were going to meet his parents or some other family thing. When they passed the house, she said nothing. It was the mystery all over again.

The way turned unfamiliar when they got a few houses down. Jonathan was talking about his father, but it was a distant thing to Emily. She had begun to feel a strange hope building in her, a strange premonition of things to come.

A new section of houses appeared bordered by a sign reading, Gideon Circle. They went into this cul-de-sac of newness. At the end, the houses gave way to woods. Emily saw this and thanked the heavens when they passed into them. She was more certain than ever of his intent and felt small butterflies begin.

The sun spilled shadows across the bank of the creek. It wasn't as deep as it could be, evident by the line of dirt along the bed where they now stood. Jonathan stopped and Emily felt her heart jump.

"We're going across. I can help you if you want."

Emily let herself be helped. She stepped into the cold water, feeling its caress on her legs. It felt good after the building heat of the day. On the other side, they climbed the embankment. At the top they walked a few more feet and exited into a field. Along the edges of it were more trees. She could see how the creek curved by the way they were growing. The clincher was the small house which stood in the center. Its worn wooden boards were ancient in the growing day.

At once she knew where they were going. His intentions were still alien to her, but she allowed herself to believe they were the intentions she wanted. She turned and saw a reflective expression on his face. He looked a million miles away.

"Are you okay?"

The look didn't falter. "I think so."

She waited for him to elaborate but he didn't. "What is this place?"

It was all it took. He supposed there were worse things that could happen. Now that it had started, there was no turning back.

A tear tracked down his face. It caught the bright sunlight and glittered as it fell away. Emily reached up to touch the small wet place it had left. "Her?"

"Yes."

The subject of his sister had come up a few days before. Jonathan was talking about someone named Arielle and Emily had to stop him and ask who she was. The story had hurt her. The faraway expression had overcome him, but no tears were shed. Jonathan had struggled with it even then. It was just too much for him now. He wasn't sure if it was the fact they were in their place or if it was his unconscious need to tell someone about it.

There was no sobbing, no loss of control, only tears. They would well, spill over and disappear. It took a few minutes of Emily hugging him to get back his composure.

"I'm sorry I cried on you."

She smiled at him, her own tears drying. "It's okay."

"I wanted to show you something."

They sat in the doorway, Jonathan talking, Emily listening. He told stories of them coming here, about scaring away the bullies, about drawings of trees, about all the things that meant so much to him. He wanted her to know everything, wanted her to know him.

She went to him then, finding his mouth and kissing him. Both were flooded by emotions so powerful they were lost to anything but the sensation. When she pulled back, both their eyes were swimming.

They decided to sit together and watch the sunset. It went slow, stretching beneath the trees and covering the world in a deep orange hue. When darkness overcame and the stars exhaled both made their way back across the moonlit field, the soft breeze of the grass careening off a young girls feet.

# Chapter Ten

Bailey Hazelwood sat up in bed. The coughing fit had been overshadowed by a hard pain in his chest that traveled up his left arm. He knew a heart attack well enough; he'd had two. The bottle of nitroglycerin was on his nightstand and he popped the cap off trying to calm the continuous coughing. He took one of the tiny white tablets and placed it under his tongue. As it dissolved, he lay back trying with all his will to calm his racing pulse. After a few minutes, the pain lessened.

It was the second time in a month he'd had to do this. The doctor said it was a possibility as weak as his heart was. The smoking didn't help, but he'd be damned if he'd give that up. Since having his first attack at fifty-three, Bailey was told he would have to be careful. He tried to for awhile but decided that if God wanted him to come on, then God would take him.

The clock said it was too early to be up and still late enough to be dark. Soft tapping resonated from the windows and the wind pulsed through the eves. The sky flashed, lighting the room and the trees beyond his window. Bailey lay on his back staring into the blackness. Each time the lightning danced, it illuminated the painting. It was a primitive thing, a still life, but it comforted him.

To say he wasn't scared would be a lie. Dying wasn't any kind of fun. It would be bad for Abbey. They weren't rich and she'd have to find some money to stick him in the ground. They'd want to put her in a home once they saw how bad she was getting.

He lit a cigar and rekindled the coughing. After a few puffs it subsided. The rain began to pick up, smacking the window harder. The sensation soothed his tired bones. Sleep wasn't coming back so he climbed out of bed. Cigar in hand he went down the stairs and crossed the foyer. He opened the front door and stepped onto the porch. He sat down on the old porch swing and let his arm rest off the back. Soft flicks of water dotted his shirtless chest.

The streets were deserted save for the occasional car. Metal street signs danced in the torrent downfall. The lighting would streak, then the dark would come back, leaving a burned image behind his eyes. It happened three times with no change to the scenery. On the forth time, he saw two silhouettes standing under the trees south of his porch.

It had been nearly a month since Jonathan had taken Emily to the field and since then, they saw each other religiously. The tirades of kisses, the long walks and constant happy mood were only part of their new found love. Everything was discovery and secrecy. They were living in a dream. Everything was bright and hopeful; there was no possibility too small. Even the barrage of a thunderstorm could do nothing to dampen their spirits

Jonathan had snuck out per Emily's request. They'd started back to school three days before and hadn't seen each other since. The plan was to sneak out after their parents were asleep and walk to the field, but the weather hadn't cooperated. The downfall was just a drizzle when they left, but by the time they got to the creek, it was a downpour.

They'd run up Baker Street trying to find familiar shelter. Jonathan's house was the closest, but it was too risky to get on the porch. They vied for a place beneath a large grouping of trees. It was still wet but no worse than the earlier drizzle.

Bailey looked on from his vantage as the boy kissed the girl and the girl kissed back. Bailey felt himself smiling. It was good to see kids in love. Hell, it was good to see anyone in love. Averting his eyes, he went back to smoking his cigar.

Jonathan had noticed Bailey's cigar on the porch,

but knew Mr. Hazelwood wouldn't tell his mother about the mysterious girl with her son. He'd been right on that too. Bailey never told anyone's business unless he had a reason to. The boy wasn't hurting anyone; he was just being a boy. It would do him good to have some happiness.

As the rain neared its end, Emily and Jonathan darted from their place beneath the trees down the sidewalk. Their laughter could be heard echoing back on the wet pavement. Bailey waited until the mists of their footfalls were nonexistent.

After an hour, he saw a silhouette coming back up the street. Jonathan's features became more recognizable the closer he came. Instead of walking to his own house, Jonathan came through the gate into Bailey's yard soaking wet.

"Out a little late aren't you?" Bailey asked.

"Yeah, thanks for pretending not to see us."

"When? When you and your girlfriend were making googles over each other behind that tree?"

"Yeah."

Bailey gave him a knowing look. "I was a boy once. I know what that's like."

Jonathan sat down. "I can't go to sleep now."

"I understand." Somewhere far away thunder rumbled. "Why you two meeting like that anyway. She's not a paroled felon is she?"

Jonathan laughed. "No."

"So what's the deal, got the lady out in the rain, soaked to the bone."

"It was her idea."

"Sounds like a fine young lady. Never could stand a girl who was afraid of a little rain."

They sat in silence. The world was beginning to cool. The wind blowing through was picking up a slight nip. "I won't tell your mama."

"I didn't think you would but..."

"Just wanted to be sure?"

"Yeah."

Bailey smiled.

"You'd better get home and into some dry clothes. Don't want to end up sick like me."

Jonathan stood, twisting his shirt. A small line of water spilled from it. "Nah, I'm still to wet behind the ears."

It struck Bailey as funny and he howled laughter. He felt the coughing wanting to rev back up again but he held it off. "Go on now before you kill me."

The old man felt he could sleep if he put his mind to it. It was still a few more hours before the sun came up. He lay on top of his sheets and continued to stare at the painting on his wall. The soft contours of the shapes within filled his mind with lazy dreams.

Jonathan was in the shower for little under five minutes, but the running water was enough to rouse his father. The knocking on the door scared him. He dropped the soap and struggled to find his voice. With his free hand, he turned off the water.

"Yeah?"

"You okay in there?"

"I couldn't sleep."

"Your mother thought you might be sick."

# JEREMY RANDOLPH

"No, I'm fine."
"Well I'm going back to bed."
"Night."
"Good-night."

Freezing, he turned the water back on. The sensation was wonderful. He wasn't sure why he hadn't told his parents about Emily. Having a girlfriend wouldn't be a big deal to them. He just felt it was more his the less people knew about it. Bailey was okay because Bailey could relate. He'd never heard a tale of his father's first love. As far as he knew, his mother was the first woman he'd ever kissed. Surely it couldn't be true but it wasn't the type of thing you brought up at dinner.

He dried off and put his sweat pants on. Vast shadows stretched up and down the hallway as he made his way. He'd never looked at the house as haunted. There was one time when he was very small that he swore he'd seen a woman standing by his bed. He'd likely been dreaming but it was enough to camp him out for weeks in his parent's room. Now, the sinister uncertainty which lingered in a dark house when the hour was long and the nights were cold was gone. All that remained was a slight mystique of silence and the loathsome call of dusk.

In his younger days, he'd known full well ghosts could exist. Known it as certainly as he knew his name, but it didn't seem like fact to him now. If there were such things as ghosts, then his sister would have undoubtedly come back to haunt him. As of yet, he'd seen no ghost.

The night stretched into daybreak and when he awoke the rain had gone. The certainty that it had fallen was evident by the humid feel of his room. His father was outside drinking coffee, the morning paper laid out across his lap. When he saw his son he looked up.

"Morning."

"Hey."

"Mom fixed some breakfast in there if you want some."

Jonathan had seen it but wasn't hungry. "Yeah, I know."

His father nodded and went back to his reading. Jonathan sat down on the chair adjacent to him.

"Where's she at?"

Again the paper went down. "Out with your aunt Sally. There's a big sale somewhere."

Jonathan leaned back. Soft coolness soaked into his shirt. His father hadn't returned the paper to its original reading position. He was continuing to look at his son.

"You up for some fishing?"

Jonathan, who hadn't been fishing with his father in at least a year, turned. "Really?"

"Sure thing. It's just the two of us today; the women won't be back for hours."

It had been ages since they'd pulled out the old boat, something they hadn't done since Arielle got sick. They were a fishing trio, so when one was out, they were all out. Now it seemed they'd be fishing partners.

# JEREMY RANDOLPH

The boat was metal and green with a small motor on the back. It was covered with an aged tarp full of leaves and water. The two pulled it back, sloshing minute fragments of the liquid onto the ground. They folded it and pulled the trailer from beneath the tree. It was an easy one man operation but his father never turned down an offer for help.

They did a quick check of its framework and found everything the way they'd left it. His father went to the shed behind the house and unlocked it. The life jackets hung on nails along the back wall. The sharp reality cut the man as he knew it would. The idea to go fishing was an attempt to get past what had happened, a feeble attempt to get back to something normal. Now, there it hung. The pink and red one picked out and adored by his lost daughter. He picked up the two jackets on either side and hung them on his arm. A thought occurred to him and the simplicity of it made him smile. He picked up the remaining jacked and carried it back outside.

Jonathan was checking the tie downs when he spied his father. He saw what the man had and understood what it meant. His father registered this and nodded. Jonathan went back to checking the gear. Once the gear was in place they guided the truck in and lined up the hitch. One last check of the harness and they headed down the driveway. They rode marveling at the lushness of the landscape. It was the peak of summer and the rain had rejuvenated all that lived. The sky broke wide with remnants of the storm clouds little more than skirts of white on the horizon.

# KINGDOM

It was a thirty mile trip and they spent most of it in silence. The meditation of the open road mixed with the reality of their absent party sucked them in. They reflected on things both past and future as they traveled the lands of their minds. They arrived at the lake and found the parking scarce. They waited for a free spot, then Jonathan climbed into the boat while his father backed it down. Once it was floating Jonathan used a paddle to push off. He'd known how to drive the motor and he had no trouble starting it now. He edged it to the dock where his father would be waiting.

With his dad in, Jonathan turned over the reins. The fishing gear was secure and the day was just beginning. With a soft turn of the handle, the boat headed out across the lake.

The wind was in his face, lapping his hair and soothing his mind. In it, he saw his sister barefoot, streaming her toes off the side of the boat. She'd be lying on her back, sunglasses in place, hair waving. She'd reach over and splash water onto him. He'd scream, try to splash back then get in trouble for moving around while the boat was moving. It was all part of the fun, the old times.

Cresting a small patch of fallen trees, they came to their fishing spot and tied off. Hooking up and spinning line, they began the ritual of choosing bait and casting off. Jonathan liked to use real worms. His father was a man of artificial tastes. They seemed to work for his father but Jonathan had never caught anything with them.

No, his bait was live bait, the kind that wiggled when you put it in the water. Twice he'd caught the winner using it, four and five pound bass. He'd needed his father's help getting them in, but in the end Jonathan alone claimed victory over their capture.

The morning sun was burning off the clouds and both felt the feel of warming skin. It was good to be back on the lake. They'd fallen into ritual easy enough but the missing member still lingered. It was this apparition that was haunting when his father's float took a jump downward.

"Dad!"

"I see it!"

His father waited a moment then snapped his wrist. The floater bobbed again and the whirring of the line broke the air.

"Feels like a big one!" He said, pulling back on the pole.

Jonathan grabbed the net.

From beneath the water, a shape appeared. It pulled towards the surface then sank away, flailing its tail trying to break free. Jonathan dipped the net beneath it.

"I bet its four pounds easy." Jonathan exclaimed as the fish came out of the water.

His father grabbed it and pulled the hook from its mouth being careful of the fins. "Whaddaya say?"

Jonathan thought about it. "Let's let him go."

His father smiled and nodded. "Yeah, I don't think your mom is up for filleting tonight." He shot Jonathan a wink and let the fish dip back into the water. Jonathan watched as the green tail disappeared into the darkness below.

"That's one for me, none for you. You'd better get in gear if you want to win today."

Jonathan, always up for a contest, went back to his pole. "You're on."

"Loser cleans the table?"

Jonathan thought about it. "And washes the dishes too."

"Ouch, that's a big wager." He faked deep thought. "Well, I am in the lead. Okay, you're on."

They shook hands and once again began the ritualistic casting and reeling. As the day wore on, his father was still up by one. Both he and Jonathan had caught something but Jonathan's was too small to eat so it didn't count. The running total was three fish. The mid afternoon heat was excruciating, but the contest was king. Only once had they stopped to eat a packed lunch. The sweet taste of bologna and cheese after hours on the water was exquisite.

They'd agreed that when four o'clock came, the endeavor would be complete. Jonathan had his line cast beside a fallen log and was willing the fish to it. Every time he thought he'd catch something, a splash would emit a few feet away from his line. He'd pull in and recast, trying to get as close to the splash as he could. Still nothing hit. He'd almost given up when something tapped his line. Trying to steady himself, he picked up the pole. His father saw this action and smiled.

"Trying to come back in the ninth, huh?"

Jonathan smiled back whispering, "Don't get too scared, it'll just be a tie."

Then the chase was on. The line snapped, Jonathan began to reel and the sounds of line coming up began. It took him a few minutes to bring it up. It was another bass, though nothing as big as the first one. It swam left and right looking for the cause of its torment. Jonathan didn't need the net to get it out. With a steady hand he removed the hook then held it up for his father to see.

"It's gonna come down to the wire isn't it?"

Jonathan nodded and looked at his watch. "An hour or so left. I'd say the next fish wins it." He bent over the boat and let the fish go. It swam away without a second thought. "Hope you like doing dishes." The sinister smile on his son's face made him laugh.

"Pretty sure of yourself now, huh? We'll see who's cleaning and who's watching TV. Age before beauty my boy. Age before beauty."

Jonathan attached a new worm and set out for the final leg of their tournament. In the end his father won, pulling in a catfish ten minutes from packing up. Jonathan took the loss in stride, even when his father began to tease him.

"I sure am gonna enjoy watching television after tonight's big meal. Too bad you'll be busy."

They packed up the gear, the tournament's outcome forgotten. It had been a good day. The fresh air of late afternoon filled their faces and cooled the tanning skin. In the end, his father would help him wash the dishes finishing the day on a high note.

# KINGDOM

By the time they reached shore, the sun was fading. They brought the boat up, tied it off and climb into the warm cab of the truck. By the time they left the lot, it was nearing dark.

They smelled of lake water and sun, a mixture of dryness and life. The air blowing from the vents was cool and refreshing. It too smelled of outdoors, the soft aroma of a million days of outside. The sound of the engine hypnotized.

It was a good thing his father offered to help him; otherwise he might have been in the kitchen all night. His mother, having come back from a large shopping trip, had invited her friend Shirley to stay for dinner. The latter had insisted on helping cook, so there was way too much content and variety.

To the delight of the chefs, both he and his father ate almost everything on the table. His mother made mention that she was glad no catfish or other such animal had made its way back into her kitchen. When her husband told her of the competition she beamed.

"Hear that Shirley? The men have cleanup duty."

Shirley, an attractive woman who was three years her senior lifted her glass. "Have fun, guys."

It took awhile to get everything straightened, but it wasn't hard work. His father washed the dishes, appointing Jonathan dryer. The two talked fishing and school, work and play. When the subject of girls came up, it was on the tip of his tongue to tell his father about Emily. Things like that hadn't been discussed outside of the harmless teasing of his youth.

"Got you a girlfriend yet?"

The question hung out there in space like an orbiting moon. "No."

"You don't sound too sure."

He wasn't sure what harm it would cause to let the secret free. His father wouldn't hound him about it and if Jonathan asked him to keep it secret, he knew he would. Still, it was something of his, a secret he shared with Emily. No matter how small the cost might be, he'd begun holding on tighter to things. This was his and his alone. No need to get the advice, ramblings and good intentions of others mixed up in it. In the end, it would only confuse him.

"No, I'm sure."

"Well when you do find one, make sure she does dishes."

"Either that or fishes better than me."

It got the two of them laughing and prompted a, "what's going on in there," from the living room.

With everything put away his father stuck his head in to see what the women were doing. They sat in front of the television with the picture on and the volume down.

"They're busy talking, let's go finish getting the gear up."

The boat was in its original position and the tarp was over it. The boxes of tackle and the life jackets still lay in front of the locked shed. His father brought out a flashlight and gathered up what he could. Arielle's jacket ended up over Jonathan's arm this time. The two went into the dark the only light small and dim.

Jonathan handed the items to his father who put them in their respective places. When he paused handing over Arielle's vest, his father touched his shoulder.

"I miss her, dad."

His father took the vest. "I do too son."

There was too much to be said and too much left to do. It was good to talk about her; they didn't do it much anymore. "She would have liked today huh?" Jonathan asked.

His father didn't speak at first. In his head his lost daughter was in the boat with them, laughing, winning the contest, doing all the little things he always took for granted, and he felt the wound open and the poisoned pain flood through him. There was more anger than tears but he held both for the benefit of his son.

"Yeah, she would have liked today." He hung the vest on the wall, flipped off the flashlight and closed the door.

# Chapter Eleven

Emily was trying to figure out what to do about Jonathan. It was three months into their quote unquote relationship and now this. Once the initial shock was over, the reality of what it meant set in. The worst was she'd known for two weeks and she'd seen him twice since then. Two times to tell him and two times she'd chickened out. It was going to be a lot for him to take in and she wasn't really sure how he'd accomplish that.

They were going to their place today. Jonathan called it that, but Emily was pretty sure he didn't mean him and her. It would be as good a time as any to get it out, purge herself of the secret she kept. When she saw his eyes, she felt her heart cry out. There was no way to do it. No way to tell him without hurting him. The worst was he had a surprise for her. Unless she was really off base, his would be a good one. One which would make the tale she must convey that much harder to express. In any event, she would dress to impress, as her mother was so fond of saying, and attempt for some degree of normalcy.

Here shirt was white and the jeans soft blue. Two small flowers sat lazily over the pockets. When Jonathan saw her, the heat once again lit. It was more than just lust. He didn't know much about that entirely but knew enough about how he felt to know it was more. There were primal feelings mixed in but the mystery of her was what made him reel, the way she said the right thing without meaning too, the way her hands would touch his. He'd never felt as alive as he did when she was around.

The backpack was secure with its contents secreted until they reached the field. Emily saw this extra article of clothing and once again found herself dreading the thing she must tell. "He's got his surprise back there so I can't see it. Some wonderful thing he wants to share with me, and what do I have for him?"

They crossed the creek and headed up the embankment. When they crested the top, Emily felt the same butterflies she'd felt the first time he'd brought her here, but they flew for a different reason now. It wouldn't be long before winter passed over the town. When it did, the travels to the field would stop. Maybe he'd tell his father about her then, when the world was asleep and there was nothing left of summer's first love. Maybe then it would be okay to let them in on his discovery, the knowledge that all things can be salvaged with love. It was such a simple idea.

Emily came up beside him and took his hand into hers. How wonderful it was to be with her. How perfect. They crossed through the doorway and into the familiar interior. Emily stood by the window looking preoccupied. Jonathan set his backpack down and unzipped the front.

"I want you to close you eyes."

Emily felt her heart skip. "Now?"

"Yes."

"Okay, but don't scare me."

"I won't."

She placed her hands over her eyes.

"I want you to sit in the doorway. I'll lead you over."

Emily let herself be led. As they went, she made a point to breath in the fragrance of his hair, the soft heat of his breath.

"Okay, when I say, open your eyes."

There was a brief pause as something shuffled.

"Okay, open them."

She did and was blinded by the light of early afternoon. As her eyes adjusted, she saw him sitting on the floor with a tablet in his hand. As understanding dawned she almost blurted out the thing she wanted to tell him.

"I'm going to need you to sit still for me."

# KINGDOM

"I thought you had a surprise for me."

"I'll have it in a little while," and he smiled so beautiful it made her heart ache.

As he looked at her, another expression washed over him. In one moment, he was the boy she'd fallen in love with; the next his face was locked in a state of total concentration. The strokes of his hand began to move with such fluidity that she could barely mark their movements. The further he went, the less she recognized him. The expression was void of anything but the task at hand. She wasn't sure he'd even notice if she got up and went outside.

Inside himself, Jonathan was in the grip of his demons. The exorcism was taking place onto the paper before him. Each stroke brought the point of his purging closer to its outcome. The face was so perfect in his normal state of reason, now in this heightened state, he thought he might go mad before he got all of it out. Each stroke went with its own accord. His conscious mind had ceased to be in control.

The image appeared on the paper as a ghost might appear in the darkest hours of twilight. It swam up out of nothing to proclaim its existence into the living world. The further it came to completion, the more amazed he would have been at its detail. Rocking back and forth he began the hair. Small intricate carvings swept this way and that as shadows gave way to light and white gave way to blackness.

Emily began to get worried when his hands began trembling. Now that he was rocking, she had half a mind to say something to him but she didn't think he would hear her if he did. She'd seen crazy people on television with the same determined look he had, people who they locked up because they'd killed their family or burned down a house full of people.

Jonathan moved from the hair to the nose, pulling the shadows up from the cheekbones. It grew towards him with each stroke of his finger. The image was now burned in his head and it didn't matter if she was there or not.

The final touches came as the wind began to pick up. It rattled through the gaps in the wood. Emily was looking west towards the line of clouds. There were soft flashes in their hearts. When she realized the movement to her left had stopped, he'd been looking at her for almost a minute. Relief washed over her as she stared into the face she associated with Jonathan. The boyish features had returned though they were hampered with slight ribbons of exhaustion.

"Finished?"

"Finished," he said.

"Can I see it?"

"If you want."

She plucked the paper from his hands and returned to the doorway. Jonathan watched as her face transformed into wonder. He'd been worried she wouldn't like it.

Emily sat looking at the image of herself. Even the face which stared back at her from the mirror wasn't as honest as this one was. He'd captured the very core of her being. It was as though she was looking at her soul, the face behind her face.

"My God," she whispered.

"Do you like it?"

"It's amazing," she said, "I've never seen anything... How do you do this?"

"Don't know. It kind of does itself."

"It's amazing."

"It's your surprise."

She ran her fingers down it. They came away black. "Thank you," and it didn't sound like enough. She went to him, covering his face with kisses. Their mouths found each other, they followed their own natural rhythm. Emily pulled away for a brief second, her blue eyes dancing. "I love you."

The words touched his ears like honey. "I love you too." It was the first time either had spoken the words. Emily looked at him, not wanting to tell him. She didn't understand why she had too. It would come to pass regardless of his knowledge of it. So what if it wasn't right? So what? This was their time and she couldn't spoil it, wouldn't spoil it. It was a good train of thought to take, but one which came too late. Jonathan had already noticed the change in her. When the dreaded question came, she found herself powerless and afraid.

"What's wrong?"

She pulled back then, not knowing what else to do. It would have to come. He'd set it into motion.

"What is it?"

Emily began to tear up, she couldn't help it. When Jonathan saw his heart sank.

"What's wrong?" He asked again.

She turned from him trying to find how to begin, how to relay the sentence with minimal pain. There was no way.

Looking at the picture in her hand, she was again struck by how perfectly he'd captured her. There was a lost look in her eyes, he'd been able to bring it out without realizing the pain behind them. When she felt his hand on her shoulder she turned, the face she loved smiling back at her, reassuring her that she could tell him anything, that they would find a way. It was enough.

"Jonathan, something's happened."

The two of them sat together in the doorway. When she began to talk, the world darkened. The clouds she'd seen in the west began to pull into Morning Ridge. Within the hour, the largest storm of the season would begin to fall, pelting the small wooden house in the center of the empty field with its endless drone of certainty. On and on she went as the rain continued to strengthen. He could stop it no more than he could stop her words.

# Chapter Twelve

It had happened the weekend before. Emily was up early when she came down the front steps and saw her father talking with a man she recognized from their days in Ohio. His name was Stanley Jenkins. Stanley Jenkins was a burly hunk of a man with broad shoulders and an even broader front. The fact that he was in the house made her stomach sink.

He was a well enough guy, educated and rich, but that wasn't cause for alarm. The problem was Stanley was in real estate. His father owned Brewster and Cambridge, an enormous real estate company with its hands in everything. It was Stanley who'd sold their house in Ohio then got them the house in Morning Ridge. Even with all that, Stanley was a friend so the alarm Emily felt would have been unjustified had she not known her mother.

Marion Brewington was a handful of a woman. The prom queen, then later Mrs. Georgia, her mother was more of a trophy than an actual person. The most intelligent thing she ever talked about was the price of this or that in relation to how much Emily's father would give her. It was about status, what she had and what she didn't have. When it came to the value of cars, jewelry, houses, Marion was on top of her game. The only issue with the constant consumption of all things new is the aftereffect her mother had been displaying for weeks, boredom. It was a well known fact that once Marion got bored, Marion got irritated. The irritation would lead to sadness, the sadness to a bitch one would be wise to steer clear of. So Marion was bored and Mr. Brewington had better fix it.

They'd come to Morning Ridge in the first place because her mother wanted to be close to nature. She'd read somewhere that the air in the rural areas was more likely to make your skin look smooth. Plus, it was the "in" thing to do. Living in the city wasn't as nice as it used to be. With that excuse in tow, Marion had given the ultimatum and once again Emily's father had agreed. It went along smoothly for awhile, but when Stanley Jenkins called one Sunday morning with news, the whole world got turned upside down.

It was all about a house. Not just any house either, a house of momentous proportions, a house owned by one of the most prominent families in St. Martin. It was the house and the location which clenched the deal for her mother. The son of the family had passed away leaving it up for auction. He'd been into drugs and had spent every dime left to him. With no remaining heirs to absorb the cost, the home went on the market.

The idea that someone else might own the very house Marion had been lusting over since she'd first seen it at twelve was a travesty. So it was Stanley who'd come to talk to Emily's father at Marion's insistence. Marion confirmed Emily's fears when one afternoon she asked, "How would like to move back to Ohio?"

Emily was unable to speak.

"Do you remember that wonderful house out by the lake? The one your grandpa used to drive us by?"

Emily did.

"Well it's going up for auction. That is unless we buy it first."

"Why would we do that?"

"Because it's the chance of a lifetime, you do realize which house I'm talking about?"

"But I like it here."

"I didn't think you liked it here."

"Well I do. I don't want to leave all my friends."

"There are boys in Ohio dear. With your looks, you'll have no trouble attracting all you want."

Her mother never went beyond the surface of anything. Emily thanked God for her father who was insightful and her grandfather who knew nothing of money until he was grown. It was their influence that had kept the far too pretty girl from becoming just another Marion.

That night in bed all she could think of was Jonathan. Beyond the small distance that parted them was what she'd always longed for. A handsome boy who didn't know or didn't care that he was handsome. A boy who's mind was an open book with hundreds of ideas for each single thing.

She'd held out hope that her father wouldn't concede but Marion had a way in the bedroom that never kept him saying no for long. So they worked out a deal with Stanley and the house would never see the auction block. The worst of it was they planned on selling their current house after they moved back to Ohio so Emily was left with the task of telling the boy she now loved, the boy who meant everything to her, that she was leaving.

Every night she searched for some elaborate way to stay. She could sleep at a friend's house, maybe set up a tent in Jonathan's back yard. In the end, there was always something that stole even the smallest hope she had of staying. It would be heartbreaking for her. She settled in for many more summers with Jonathan. Sometimes she'd wake and think it was a dream. No moving van with its hydraulic screams to rouse her. No men pulling out sofas and tables, tearing down in hours the things which took years to grow accustomed to.

As they sat silent, Jonathan felt the coldness he'd tried so long to still, blink on. The rain strengthened, as if understanding the magnitude of the situation, and began leaking onto the dusty floorboards. The picture he'd draw was too close to the wetness and she moved it in closer.

"Say something."

Jonathan wasn't sure he could, wasn't sure that if he opened his mouth he wouldn't wound her. Say something to the effect of, "Well go on then, get the hell out. I don't need you anyway," but it wasn't true and he knew it.

"No chance they'll change their minds?" His words were strained but they were a welcomed sound to her ears.

"I don't think so."

He took her hand. "What are we going to do?"

It was the "we" that melted the fear from her. That one word and the solitude was gone. "I don't know. "

Jonathan searched his mind. When nothing presented itself he kissed her hand. "When?"

"Next Friday."

It was out, set in concrete. There was a date and a destination. He stared at the light shining from the cracks in the roof. Emily slid in beside him. They sat that way listening to the storm as it passed over them, Jonathan drunk on her scent, the sweet smell of her breath and the feel of her hair against his cheek.

When the rain began to taper, Emily lifted her head and looked at him. "Think we'd better get back?"

It wasn't coming down in torrents as it had been, but it was coming down enough. Emily picked up her picture and took it to him.

"Put this in your pack, I don't want it to get wet."

He did. "I'm gonna count to three, then we'll go for it. One."

Before he could get to two she kissed him. "I'm sorry about everything."

He stared down into her timeless face. "Don't be."

They took off across the field, the soaked ground splashing muddy spouts of water. It didn't take long to reach the edge. Emily started over the embankment meaning to slide down and head across. Jonathan grabbed her by the shoulders and pulled her back. Her feet went out from under her and she landed hard on her bottom.

"What are you doing?" She started to ask, but stopped. The ground was gone. Where it was, a flood of brown water was racing by.

"I would have been swept away."

Jonathan sat beside her. "I'm sorry if I hurt you."

Emily didn't look at him. "I'm ok, but how are we going to get across that?"

What was once a three foot bank was gone. "We can't until the water drops."

"How long does that take?"

"Could take all night."

"What are we going to do?"

"Go back."

Their place was as they'd left it, but now they were soaked to the bone. They got back against the furthest wall trying to keep out of the wind.

"What do you think your parents will do when you're not back by curfew?" Jonathan asked.

"Mom probably won't notice." she said through chattering teeth. "Dad's not home tonight."

"My mom's probably on the porch yelling for me."

Emily laughed at that. "I'd like to meet her if we get the chance. She seems nice."

"Yeah, she's okay. Do you mind eating around people?"

"No."

"Well, maybe you could come by for dinner."

Emily was the first to fall asleep. Too many nights of worry had finally caught up with her. The rain tapered as the morning approached. When the sun drifted in, Jonathan opened his eyes. Fingers touched his cheek and he looked down to see her staring back at him. Her eyes were still sleepy, but he thought she looked rejuvenated.

"I thought it would take a little longer before we slept together."

Jonathan kissed her forehead. "I guess I'm just easy."

"Feels warm." She stretched her arms and groaned with the sensation. "Think the creeks back to normal?"

"I hope so, mom's gonna kill me. The police are probably out searching the streets."

"Tell her she can't ground you until after next Friday."

"It wouldn't stop me if she did."

They got up, Jonathan doing his own stretching, and headed outside. It was warmer with the sun on their faces and they reveled in the sensation. There was no need to run now so they settled into a walk. The canopy green but the first signs of orange was creeping in.

"It'll be pretty out here in a few months." Emily said following his eyes. "If I was still here, we could rake up all those and have a big time jumping into them."

It was a simple enough comment but one that reaffirmed the reason he was so drawn to her. They were two of the same kind, two spirits with the same winds in their sails.

They went into the trees, brushing water down from the leaves as they did. The creek was not back to its original size but it was down enough to cross. The worst they could do was fall in and get wet again. When they got to the other side he heard the sound of a zipper.

"Don't think I'm gonna let you take this back do you?"

Jonathan smiled and stood still so she could extract her picture from his backpack. She was amazed all over again at the image staring back at her. "You know, no matter what, I'll keep this forever."

It took awhile to reach her house. The door was closed and the front porch light still on. If Emily was lucky, her mother would have gone to bed before she came home and would still be sleeping.

"Time to face the music."

Emily smiled. "Yeah, I'm not sure if it'll be too loud though. Mom's probably sleeping."

"Lucky you."

"You do realize you're spending every day I have left with me."

"Yes."

"Your mom gonna kill you?"

"I have no doubt." A ghost of a smile creased his face.

"Well get home then boy, don't want to be a bad influence." She gave him a quick kiss, watchful of the ever present prying eyes of the neighborhood. "Call me later, okay?"

"Sure."

The walk to his own house was much quicker than a snail's pace, it was a flat out run. Once the drug had been taken from him, the reality set back in. There was no chance his parents were still asleep. No chance that they'd gone to bed early sure of the fact their boy would be home safe. There were too many dark crevices to the world and both his parents knew it.

It was his father who saw him first, standing on the stairs dressed in blue jeans with his hair unkempt. There was a look of relief when he saw Jonathan. He hailed his father, one hand up. The man didn't wave back. By the time he was close enough to touch his father scooped him up and hugged him hard.

"Where have you been? I've been up all night looking for you."

"I got stuck on the other side of creek."

"You know to come back across before a storm comes in; what was so important you couldn't come home?"

The thing he'd been keeping now seemed appropriate. It didn't matter anyway, everything had changed. "Emily."

"Who?"

"Emily Brewington."

Understanding dawned on his father's face. The look of unconscious concern began to slip away. "A girl, huh?"

Jonathan nodded.

"This is the first I've heard of it."

"I don't like to talk about it."

"How long has this been going on?"

"A few months."

"A few months?" His father sounded surprised and strangely elated. "Keeping secrets from your old man? Do you like her?"

"Yes, sir."

"Does she like you?"

"Yes."

"Well it sounds like you have it made in the shade. Far as I can see, you only have one problem."

Jonathan gave a questioning glance.

"Your mother."

"I know, I'm sorry. We were talking and the time got away from me. We tried to come back, but it was just too deep."

"Well I'm glad you had some good judgement. How about her parents? Did you get her into trouble?"

"No, her mother was asleep I think. Her dad's out of town."

"Sounds like she got off luckier than you."

Behind him the screen door swung open and his mother descended on him. "Don't you ever do that to me again!" She pulled him from his father and began hugging him.

Jonathan let himself be hugged, "I'm sorry."

"Where were you?"

Jonathan started to explain, trying to find the best method to convey what had happened, but his father took the lead.

"He got rained in on the wrong side of the creek and had enough sense not to try and cross."

"The creek?"

"You know, the one down by Gideons."

"What were you doing down there?"

"I was just..,well."

"He was just taking some time to himself, lost track of time and was smart enough not to get himself drowned."

His mother processed this, saw the logic and the good judgement in her son's actions, then looked back at him. "I don't want you going down there anymore. It's too dangerous and you could get hurt."

"But mom..."

"I want you to promise me."

Before he could lie to her, his father intervened again. "I think it's best we all go in and get some breakfast. Your decision wasn't the best, but it was better than getting hurt by trying to come home."

# JEREMY RANDOLPH

His mother looked at him. The excitement in her eyes had been replaced by reassurance. "Are you hungry?"

"Starved."

They went back inside, the fear and desperation fading from all but Jonathan. Emily would be leaving soon and all the ramifications of what it meant would soon come. He recognized it for what it was, the knowledge of another love gone, and though he welcomed the time he had left, he knew it would be only make it worse when the time finally came.

He felt his mother's hand in his hair and looked up into her dark eyes. He understood then that he had become an object to her as well, a thing too easily lost, and it filled him with a sense of isolation. To them he was theirs, and while that was true, the desperate need to hold on to him made him want to break free. His mother smiled and he smiled back, hopeless in this new understanding.

# Chapter Thirteen

It was Wednesday after the all night incident that first gave birth to an idea. The brilliance of it was so simplistic that Jonathan couldn't believe he hadn't thought of it already. Maybe there was something he could do to keep Emily there.

The first step was to retrieve a certain item from Arielle's room. The old tin of brushes was pushed so far back in her dresser drawer, it was almost invisible. Jonathan withdrew the smallest of these and stuck it behind his ear. Elation once again washed over him. The thought that Emily could stay, even if it was a long shot, was wonderful.

Mr. Hazelwood's front gate flew back as Jonathan crossed into the yard. The door was open but the screen was closed. He knocked on it and stepped back. After a second he tried again. This time he heard footsteps. It wasn't Bailey, but Abigail that came to the door. She looked healthy but confused.

"May I help you?"

"Yes, I'd like to talk to your brother, is he home?"

"Ronald?"

"No, ma'am Bailey."

"Bailey? Why, I believe he's upstairs, a little under the weather today."

"May I speak with him?"

She considered. Jonathan waited until her gaze returned to him. "What? Oh yes, Bailey. Let me see," and she disappeared down the hall.

Jonathan walked to the edge of the porch and sat. He would be cutting it short. Emily would be gone in less than a week. The door opened and Jonathan turned. Bailey came out moving slow.

"What brings you by?"

"Well, I wanted to ask you something."

Jonathan saw the old man's eyes go to the brush behind his ear. "Wanted to ask me something, huh?"

"Yes, sir."

"I think I understand." Bailey said. "It's not time for that now. Not yet."

"Can I at least plead my case?"

"If you want."

Jonathan began to talk. Mr. Hazelwood listened.

"She's leaving Friday. Her parents are making her go."

"And she doesn't want to go, wants to stay with you?"

"Yes. We've tried everything. When I remembered your story about Camille, it was perfect. It's the same thing, can't you see it?"

"It was a different world then."

Jonathan felt anger rise but pushed it back. "I understand that I love her and I don't want her to go."

Bailey nodded, feeling slow and worn out. "Jonathan, you could lose her inside the magic."

"Then why did you tell me about it?"

Bailey didn't want to get into it with him. Weeks of bed rest had done nothing to calm the intensifying fatigue he felt. He still hadn't come to terms with his own decision to give up the jars.

"About a year before your sister died, she came to me wanting to know about drawing. I'd told her the story of my painting. She said you had been drawing and that you were good. I guess she thought I was an old hat at it. Whatever the case, she brought me something you'd done. It was a bird, a sparrow. I remember thinking how good you must be. Then she got sick and we never spoke about it again. For whatever reason, Camille entrusted me with these things. I spent countless hours trying to figure out how to unlock their potential, the only problem was I wasn't very good. I managed to harness the correct mix of emotion and talent a few times, but each was a disaster. When it almost killed me, I stopped. I hid the jars and haven't used them sense."

"Give them to me. I can figure them out. I am good, I can make it work." Jonathan heard the desperation in his own voice and fought to control it.

"When your world has settled down a bit, you'll understand. It's not your place to use what I offer for this. If you can find another way to keep your girlfriend here, I suggest you use it. Otherwise, you must tell her goodbye and move on."

Jonathan could no longer hold the emotions. They broke without reason or meaning. "Please. I need her here. I don't have anything else."

And Bailey almost gave in. He felt himself longing to still the boy's pain. Hadn't he been through enough already? It was that thought that stood him firm. Jonathan didn't understand what it meant to have the jars. Bailey hoped that he lived long enough to tell him the full truth. If the good Lord took him before the tale was told, the boy would be no less for it. The secret would die with him and in the end maybe that would be enough.

"I'm sorry." Bailey said.

Jonathan tried to be angry with him, but in the end he couldn't bring himself to do it. Bailey had never done anything to hurt him; in fact, he had given Jonathan the first hope of life after Arielle died. Maybe he wouldn't be able to control the magic, maybe it would hurt Emily. The thought cooled the anger and softened his heart back to the familiar normality he associated with living, sadness.

# KINGDOM

Jonathan hopped off the porch and walked back through the gate. The day was just beginning, but already he felt like he'd been up for hours. He could feel the old winding down of the atmosphere, the sullen calming of the internal works. Once Friday passed, he feared what was to come.

Emily came out at four that evening. She was dressed in a yellow dress with a matching flower barrette in her hair. Each day closer they came to her departure, the more beautiful she seemed to him. The walk was quiet, both were trying too hard to remember every moment of it.

The dinner his mother had prepared was larger than the one she and Shirley had done after their infamous fishing trip.

Jonathan stood with Emily at the front door.

"You think they'll like me?" She asked.

"Nah, they'll throw bread at you."

She hit his arm.

"You ready?"

The smile fell away. "Yes." And she kissed him. She hadn't planned on doing it. It might have been the way he was looking at her. It could have been the sudden realization that she wouldn't have much time left to do it in. Whatever the reason, it felt good.

The sound of metal twisting and seams pulling alerted both and they pulled back. It was Jonathan's father. In one hand he held the newspaper, in the other a used napkin. He had his reading glasses on and they reflected the warm light of the house. The smell of baking wafted out in fragrant streams.

"I heard you out here stomping around, thought you might like to come inside."

Emily smiled and took a step forward.

"Dad, Emily, Emily, Dad."

"Hello." His father said, repositioning the paper under his arm. "Good to meet you."

They found Jonathan's mother bent over a pan of boiling noodles, her back too them. When her husband poked her, she spun, startled.

"You trying to kill me?" Then she saw the company and composed herself. "Is this the famous Emily?"

"Yes ma'am."

His mother crossed to where the girl stood, hands folded in front of her.

"Jonathan has told me a lot about you." Emily said.

Jonathan's mother looked at him. "Well at least someone is up on their information. I just heard of you two days ago." Jonathan ignored the put-out look his mother shot in his direction.

"I kept telling him there's no reason to be ashamed of me." Emily said and gave her own look towards the boy.

Jonathan shrugged. "I can't help it. I'm a shroud of secrecy."

"I hope you like chicken, I know these boys do, but us girls are fickle sometimes."

"No ma'am, I like chicken."

"And such manners, I like this one Jonathan, she's a keeper." Then as if realizing what she said, "who wants to help mash the potatoes?"

Jonathan's father, who had sat down to read the paper, looked up. The comment had been intended for him alone.

It was strange to see his mother in such a good mood. Most days the haze of life without Arielle overshadowed anything else about the normally vibrant woman. The two had shared countless secrets and pains, their friendship one of the most important pieces of his mother's life.

"Jonathan put ice in the glasses."

The dinner drifted in the way only dinner with good friends and family can. The conversation was light and easy, the food wonderful. Sometimes someone would ask a question, usually one about Emily's past. The girl would do her best to answer while chewing a mouthful of potatoes. By the time the desert was brought, both Jonathan's mother and father had decided they liked the girl.

When it was over the two kids excused themselves. The "thank yous" and the "good to meet yous" flew as they always did in such a situation. With the formalities complete and the divergence from everyday life at an end, Jonathan and Emily walked back into the world which was theirs alone, the open air.

They were halfway down the street before Emily decided to say something. Too much wanted to spill out and she didn't know where to start. "I like your mom."

"Yeah, I could tell she likes you."

"How?"

"She was smiling."

Two more days, and they would be void of each other, purged of the companionship neither had asked for, but now could not comprehend losing. They walked the length of Baker Street heading north instead of south. The hanging trees shadowed their features as they moved mindless of any direction or reason.

"You know, you'll still be able to call me and stuff."

"Yeah."

"Maybe even come visit."

Jonathan had bent his own mind around these things many times, but he wasn't a stupid boy. Time was many things, the most poignant being a changer. Once they were outside of this world, they would have to become something else to survive. One day the something else would become unfamiliar. It was as if the people they were had disappeared. The apparition standing before you might be the body you remember, but the spirit housed within could be as different as night and day, an imposter posing as a memory.

But it wasn't fair to get mad at her about it. The same thing would happen to him. It had in fact already begun to happen. Not six months ago, he was obsessed with loss and the emotions it foretold. Now he'd met a beautiful girl. They would continue, but to what end? He didn't know. All that mattered was that she was there, a tangible thing. Projecting into the future, he could see the nights when he'd think of her, long to touch her, and find she too was gone.

As if reading these thoughts she gripped his hand. "Where are we going?"

"I want to show you something."

They crossed to the enormous tree towering high above the town. Emily looked up at it and for a moment confused.

"Can you climb?"

The look she returned made him sorry he'd asked. The lighthearted beauty returned and she reached up. In seconds, she was rising through the branches.

Emily stopped at the perfect parting of the limbs. It was easy to see why he loved to come up here. The view was breathtaking. Beyond the ridge she could see lights spread over a vast distance. She wasn't sure where they were coming from, but she didn't think it mattered.

"I've had fun," she said.

"Yeah, the food was good."

"Not just tonight, all of it."

"Me too."

"Think we're gonna make it through this?"

Jonathan searched his heart for an honest answer. He owed her that much. "I don't know."

She smiled. "It'll be interesting."

They sat there for the rest of the night, the lights of the houses flickering in the silent distance. It didn't matter that the world was getting ready to change again. Both could feel it coming like a snake in the shadows. Yet there was nothing they could do.

"Whatever happens, I won't forget you. Promise you won't forget me."

Jonathan let the impact of the words run through him. He could feel the love for her burning bright in his veins. "How could I forget you?" And with it said, he kissed her. It was the first time he'd been so bold. She let herself be kissed, knowing it was love she felt for him, love so unmistakable that she wasn't sure she could live without it.

# Chapter Fourteen

When the final day came, Jonathan crested the hill and saw the bright yellow moving van. Three men were going in and out of it carrying furniture and boxes. Emily was in the house trying to make sure she'd gotten everything packed. When she looked up and saw him, sadness washed over her. "I don't want to go. It's not fair."

Jonathan felt deep and sudden anger flair towards Bailey. If he'd only given him what he wanted. Then she was kissing him, the taste of her tears flooded his mouth.

Downstairs rustling footsteps and unfamiliar

voices coated the air with unconscious urgency. Everything was alive with change, but neither of them felt it. Then someone was in the room with them. There was a clearing throat then more movement. The large man with the words, 'Hampton Movers', on his shirt stepped around them and began breaking down what was left of Emily's bed. They continued to look at each other, so close he could feel her breath on his skin.

"It's not goodbye." Jonathan said.

Emily thought she knew better. "I know."

"We'll see each other again, maybe I'll come down to and visit you."

In the quiet of morning they stood, tears drying on their faces. It had come to an end. A point in time where there was no way to stop forward. Everything would spin out from that point, a marker on the road of their lives.

Jonathan did his best to help. There were a few boxes that needed to go, and a few glass things Emily didn't trust herself to carry. By afternoon, the truck was loaded and it was time for the real goodbye.

White smoke rose as the diesel engine idled. Emily's parents sat in their car waiting for their daughter, the house behind them looming like a ghost.

"I'll call you as soon as we get settled, let you know my new address and stuff."

"Okay."

"It was a good time wasn't it?"

"Yeah."

She pulled him to her one last time. "You're pretty

cute when you're sad." The tears wanted to start but she held them back.

"Until next we meet remember, I love you."

Emily hugged him fiercely. "I love you to, I hate this."

"It'll be okay."

Then they were apart. It happened like a dream. Emily walked away from him; then she was in the car. The large van fell into gear, engine revving. Emily began to wave as the car pulled off from the curb. Jonathan stood as another part of his life disappeared into the afternoon.

When there was no physical glimpse remaining he turned to the house. The windows were all naked, the curtains gone. It looked like a shell to him, a coffin with no life inside. The soul was gone, purged of its existence. It was nothing now but a reminder of things that could have been and things that may never be again.

Hands in his pockets, he made his way towards home. By the time he went to bed that night the retracting darkness had once again closed in. Days fell in front of him like timeless holes.

It was the same in the house next door to him. Things were beginning to slip lose and give way. Bailey had seen the van pulling away from his bedroom window. He'd watched the boy return from the pain that was becoming his defining feature. The regret of his decision wasn't fresh, but somewhere in the back of his mind he wondered if he'd done the right thing.

## JEREMY RANDOLPH

There was a pad of paper in the nightstand beside his bed. He took it out and thumbed to a clean sheet. A black pen lay beside his lamp and he picked it up. Words didn't come as easy as they once did, but he would write just the same. The rock of the message was what mattered, not the elegance of the grass around it. It took an hour or so to finish, but in the end, it was enough. He folded it, putting it in the only place he knew no one would look. With its secrecy contained, he again tried to sleep. With some surprise, he found it easier than expected.

Jonathan woke late the next morning. He knew Emily would be in her new house and he hoped he would get a call from her. He didn't. It took three days for the phone to ring. When it finally did, he was outside helping his father. His mother's voice carried and he knew at once what it meant.

The receiver was still in her hand and he snatched it without notice of his mother's surprise.

"Hello?"

"Hey there!"

The sound of her voice was wonderful.

"I thought you'd forgot about me."

"This soon? Not a chance."

"So how are you liking it out there?"

"Oh, it's okay. A few of my old friends came by to say hello. Things sure are different."

"I bet."

"So what are you doing?"

"Nothing much, I was helping dad cut down that dead tree out back."

"The one we thought would fall if we leaned against it?"

"That's the one."

"Too bad, I liked that tree."

Silence.

"I miss you." It was Jonathan speaking.

"I miss you too. The guys around here are all retarded. Do you know one of them already tried to ask me out?"

Jonathan felt a shot of fire hit his chest.

"I said no though, I don't know what he was thinking."

"Yeah."

"I can't talk too long, mom is having a fit about the phone bill. I wanted to give you my address though, and my new number. Go get a pen, boy."

Jonathan smiled and went to the kitchen drawer. A small collection of what he needed was inside. "Okay, go ahead."

Emily began speaking and he wrote with precision. Any loss of information could result in detrimental communication breakdown. Before he could go on to an other subject, he heard a woman's voice in the background.

"My mom says she needs to use the phone. Can I call you back later?"

"Yeah." A pause. "I'm glad you got there okay."

"Me too. I'll talk to you later."

"Bye."

"Bye."

There was a click and she was gone.

# JEREMY RANDOLPH

He waited for the phone to ring all night. He waited the next day too. After three days, he called her. Her friends were over and the conversation was strange. They had begun to change without the other, the distance creating an odd breed of confusion and jealousy. They tried hard to sustain the connection, but time was a destroyer. The final break came two months after she'd settled in. A boy named Matthew had asked her to the movies.

"I kissed him." It fell on Jonathan's ears and broke his mind. It was as if the whole world had turned black. No longer did he hear the warmth in her voice. She was pulling away for good this time.

"We can't keep on like this, I'll always love you, but I want to remember the old times. You understand right?"

Jonathan had hung up the phone. No 'good-byes', no 'I love yous' just a simple action. All that was good was gone. An hour later, he stood beside the creek he'd taken her to so long ago. With shaking hands, he tore up the small scrap of paper that held her phone number, address, and her name. The tiny pieces drifted into the water and were washed downstream. Then, without reason, he walked into the current and lay down.

The cold pierced his skin, tearing the breath from his lungs and quickening his heart. Above, the parted canopy of sky shone through in a deep aqua hue. He lifted his feet.

Small patches of rock nipped his back. The rushing greens and blues bore the sensations of pain from his mind. He was in a state of pure isolation, purging himself of whatever life he had left. It was the release of his will. The stream would carry him by its own accord. There was no reason to fight it anymore. Whatever wounds it inflicted would come as they would and he would accept them graciously. It was no longer in him to try and control anything.

As the water got deeper the tiny stings passed bringing stranger ones of weightlessness. The current began to pick up and he felt himself turning around backwards. He passed beneath an overpass, and for a moment the sky was gone. Then he emerged on the other side. He was going to sleep. It was a strange thing to realize but it was true.

In the naked limbs above, a crow watched the boy drift. It called out in a shrill voice. The boy's eyes didn't open; he was lost in the blessed darkness. The bird cawed once more and flew off towards the north.

For most of the afternoon, Jonathan drifted. From time to time he'd come awake, blink against the blazing sun, and disappear back into darkness.

When he stopped moving, cool wind was blowing in his face. He opened his eyes and found the blue sky was gone. What replaced it were a million pin points of light. He sat up, aware that he wasn't moving anymore, and did a quick check of his surroundings. Nothing was familiar.

The water wasn't deep so he crossed and climbed the embankment. He wasn't surprised to see he had no idea where he was. There was no street or houses, only woods. He briefly considered following the creek back but decided against it. Backtracking wasn't what he wanted. Coming this far was good. Besides he didn't care what happened. No more worries about parents or consequences. He'd gone into the unknown willingly.

Walking in the woods at night brought its own challenges, the trees blocked what little light he had to see by and he had to move with his hands out to keep from running into anything. It was raw out here, as raw as him. There were no apologies, no maps, no hopes, no dreams, just existence. Nature didn't need anyone around making sure that everything was working properly. Whatever the world was, it had been set into motion, and it would continue in that motion until it burned up against itself. It brought back the hesitant thought that there was no here after, that when you left, you left alone into the black and into the dust.

He felt cold. The thought of Arielle lying beneath the earth, taken over by the very thing that consumed him. The endless movement of the natural world, the one thing that cared not about the pretty pink dress she was buried in, nor the water spilling in to soil it. The rot of bacteria and time would strip away her beautiful face, leaving holes of black liquid sliding into the perfect satin of the coffin. There was a lie going on, a fabrication of the truth. It seemed everybody cut down the trees and the things which grew without care because they were a reminder of their own existence but Jonathan was becoming aware that he wasn't so much different than the spider, weaving a web to catch its food, night after night, relentless. That was the real truth, so apparent to him now that he didn't understand why he'd never seen it before. Dear God, what consequences it meant.

An hour after he'd begun his trek into the dark, he began to hear the sounds of the highway. He didn't move towards it, but kept it to his left, occasionally seeing distant lights through the trees. Eventually, the woods began to thin as he came to houses. He'd been moving straight and felt no reason to deviate so within minutes he was crossing into people's yards. They were all cut, little patches of green around luminescent homes which though beautiful, were not approachable. He crossed a side yard and onto asphalt.

He recognized the road by the landmarks and signs. It was the highway that stretched towards the interstate and into places he'd never seen. He walked three miles before the sun rose.

The traffic began to strengthen as commuters filed out to start the day and he did his best to stay out of view. When he heard the rustle of tires on gravel, he knew someone was pulling up behind him. He assumed it would be a policeman, but when he recognized the voice, he turned.

Father Mason stood looking at the boy with concern.

"What are you doing way out here, Jonathan?"

Jonathan didn't speak.

"Son, are you all right?"

Jonathan looked at the man but said nothing.

"Can I give you a ride home?"

"Don't wanna go home."

"Your mama is probably worried about you."

"I'm sure."

"So what's the problem here?"

"No problem, I'm just going for a walk."

"You do realize you're about fifteen miles outside of town?"

Jonathan, who didn't care if he was a hundred miles outside of town, said nothing.

"I can't leave you out here alone, either you come with me or I'll have to get the police."

Jonathan saw there was no way out. He walked past Father Mason and opened the door to his truck. He put on his seat belt and sat looking out the window.

Father Mason tried twice to get conversation going, but Jonathan wasn't in the mood. He gave up trying and focused on getting him home. His parents were concerned too, more from his attitude than his appearance, but they were just glad he wasn't hurt. Jonathan walked to his room, blood still drying on his tired body, and didn't come out all day.

As night fell and everyone went to sleep, he sat down on the floor. In his right hand was Arielle's notebook. The last page set quiet, the final piece in yet another tale. Holding it so the light would catch, he began to read, reveling in his sister's words and letting go of yet another broken anchor.

"Don't know how much longer I can keep this up. The last round of chemo made my hair fall out. The doctor says there's no reason to keep trying it. I should go home and try to live the rest of my life. I suppose this will be the last time I see the inside of this place.

# KINGDOM

Jonathan isn't with me today; he's gone with mama to run some errands. I wanted to make peace with everything alone. I didn't want to make him sad.

I suppose I've lived a good life, I had a lot of happy times. I won't say that this is fair and I won't say that I understand why it happened. Things don't always make sense. I've tried so hard not to get angry but I'm not so good at it anymore. I don't want to die. It's just not fair. There is so much I won't be able to do, so many things I wanted to experience. The hospice lady they sent out last week, Ms. Wisdom, says I should reflect on the good things I've done and try to give as much love to my family as I can, make memories with them. It's a good speech but I don't want to be a memory. Memories fade.

I don't know if anyone will ever read this, or if Jonathan will find the strength to come out here and get it after I'm gone. If you have Jonathan and your reading, then I'm already gone. I want you to know that I still love you and, if there's something after this, I'll be thinking about you and mama and daddy. Tell them I said so.

It's time to go home now. This is Arielle Constance Murray signing off."

# Part II
Salvation

# Chapter Fifteen

Five years passed between Emily's leaving and the day Mr. Hazelwood was carried out of his home on Baker Street on a stretcher. It was the second time that year one of the occupants had been brought out by someone else's devices. The previous year the coroner had carried out Abbey. She'd died in her sleep. Bailey was lucky, if you wanted to call it lucky. The people carrying him out were from Bountiful Living Retirement Home.

It was a beautiful day. The sun burned hard brilliance into his eyes and the old man did his best to shield them from it. He hadn't been outside in over a week, his back kept him from moving around much, and when he'd run out of food he'd called the grocery to ask for a delivery. They'd sent a young man who reported back to his supervisor about Bailey's condition. The man was concerned about the boy's story and took it upon himself to call the sheriff. When he showed up, Bailey was barely able to walk.

Jonathan hadn't spoken to him in ages. It was the first time he'd had seen him all summer. Sitting on the steps trying to finish the book his teacher had assigned, Jonathan noticed the ambulance. He'd taken to stealing glances every few minutes to see what was going on. When he saw Bailey, he hardly recognized him.

He wore an oxygen mask and appeared hard pressed for air. His tangled white hair whipped in the ever present breeze. Jonathan stared unbelieving at how thin his old friend had become. He felt a sharp pang of guilt at the sight. How long had it been since they'd talked, a year? It had been at least that.

The stretcher struck the edge of the ambulance and Bailey looked over and found Jonathan's eyes. The expression was one of patience, one that said it was okay he hadn't come to see him, he understood. Again, guilt resonated. It wasn't normal for Jonathan to be feeling bad about something. It was a grand day when he felt anything at all.

He sat the book aside and tried to smile at Bailey. The man seemed to register the effort and tried to smile back. Then the doors were closing, the engine was running, and the sound of sirens began. Jonathan watched as they disappeared down Baker Street. The old house next door peered at him with cold isolation.

At dinner, Jonathan sat with his parent's eating pizza. It was a rare occasion when his mother would cook now and an ever rarer one when Jonathan would eat with them. His father was on the verge of a punch line which had his face red and his voice rising in an odd octave of girlish laughter. Despite himself, Jonathan was being pulled into the hilarity.

"Oh man, the boy might smile."

Jonathan was about to do just that when the roar of the telephone broke. Jonathan reached back and picked up the receiver, passing it to his mother. She said hello, began to listen, and the fun melted from her face. Then the receiver was returned to him. Jonathan hung it up and waited.

"They've put Mr. Hazelwood in a retirement home."

"Oh no." It was his father speaking. The tone was solemn but not surprised.

"He put us down as his next of kin."

She looked at Jonathan and he shrugged. "He doesn't have anybody else."

"What else did they say?" his father put in.

"They're going to auction his house to help pay for the medical bills."

The idea angered Jonathan. "I'm glad their first priority is how an old man is gonna pay."

"Well at least he won't have to be alone anymore."

Jonathan wasn't sure if his mother had meant to

say something without coming out and saying it. She'd known about his visits to Bailey and had welcomed them. When he stopped she didn't put up much fuss about it, though she had voiced disapproval on more than one occasion.

Jonathan didn't favor her with a response and went on eating his pizza.

"They said he had a message for you."

It caught him off guard. "Me?"

"There are some things he wants you to get for him."

"Why doesn't he get someone else to do it?"

"Because he asked you."

"Did he say what?"

"Some personal things from his bedroom, pictures and such."

"That's it?"

"Why, did you expect something else?"

"No, not really."

"Well he said you knew where the spare key was. Just bring the pictures from his bedroom and anything else you might think he'd want. We'll take it over to him this weekend."

The next day Jonathan woke and got dressed. He wasn't looking forward to going back into Bailey's house, especially without the old man there. He shook it off and made his way across the front yard. The key was under a stone flanking the door. Jonathan retrieved it and unlocked the door. The smell of age and emptiness wafted out.

Bailey hadn't been gone physically for long, but

# KINGDOM

he'd stopped tending to things much further back. There were dishes in the kitchen with old food and a few glasses of turned milk. The little bit of light that managed to peek through the drawn windows showed showers of dust in its wake.

The stairs groaned under his weight. The light from the kitchen faded as clouds moved across the sky. It made him sad to be here, to be having to do this for his old friend. Bailey shouldn't have to end up dying in some brightly lit, sterile environment. The man had been great once, sound of mind and with more integrity than Jonathan had ever known. Yet the whole thing added to his belief that in the end you always end up alone.

The door was open and the bed pulled down. Feeling out of place, he went to the task at hand. There were three pictures beside the bed. Jonathan recognized the woman in one as Abigail. The others were mostly yellowed images with white borders around the edges with people he didn't recognize.

The bag his mother insisted he bring was slung over his shoulder and he placed the pictures inside. There were a few more hanging on the wall, one of a woman, the other of a still life. He grabbed them and scanned the room for anything else. Satisfied he'd gotten everything important he went back downstairs stopping long enough to pluck a few more pictures from the wall.

Outside the air was fresher. The pack on his back was heavy. In his mind's eye he saw the old man sitting on the steps, a large cigar in his hand. He felt guilty standing there with Bailey's things. Had he been wrong to be angry? He wasn't sure. Mr. Hazelwood had always been kind to him, had always been kind to his whole family when it came down to it. The only thing Jonathan ever did for him was shun him, avoid him, try to get something from him, and when he wasn't given it, ignore him.

Pulling the door to, he crossed to the sidewalk. Once the auction came so would a new family. It would be strange seeing some other group of people living in the house he'd always associate with Bailey and Abbey. The setting of his life was going through another structural change. The idea occurred to him that eventually everything in the world would reissue itself. It reminded him of something they'd learned in biology, the fact that the human body rebuilds itself many times as it grows. It's still the same body, same things inside, but there's still something new. He supposed the world was a little like that. The houses along the street would stay, the trees would grow taller. The concrete would crack but still remain. The houses would be re-inhabited by families until the entire landscape of his childhood memory was altered. The props would stand but the players would go. The true world existed in his mind. There and only there were things as they should be. It made him sad to realize, but it wasn't entirely new. He became aware of change long before his epiphany on the porch.

When he got home, his mother packed Bailey's things into a cardboard box, wrapping each so they wouldn't break. When the intricacies of this were

# KINGDOM

done, she sealed it. It sat by the front door until Saturday. Jonathan been given the task of taking it to Mr. Hazelwood. His mother thought it best he should go alone. She thought Jonathan had been way too quiet since retrieving the items and thought there might be some unfinished business between the two.

He secured the box in the seat next to him and put the seat belt on it for good measure. Being he was a good foot taller than his mother, he spent the first few minutes adjusting mirrors and the seat. Once satisfied, he started it up. His mother stood on the porch watching all this and when Jonathan looked up, she waved. He waved back then spun around to back up.

As the town wound out around him, he again felt the sense of freedom he always associated with being alone. No one could reach him. The radio was factory but still packed a good sound. Jonathan rolled past his mother's easy listening and honed in on a rock station. The sound filled the interior giving life to the journey ahead. As he sang the words to himself, he rolled down the window and let the wind fill his senses. He continued that way, one arm resting in the open breeze.

Once outside of town, the landscape became rows of cornfields. They stretched to the sky, tall, green and wavering. He was on his way to Hilltop, a small community west of Morning Ridge. He'd only been there once, a long time ago, with his father. There wasn't much for the young in the town. It consisted of a hospital, a handful of retirement homes, and the local shops and markets. If Jonathan wanted to go somewhere, he'd usually head east towards Towers Landing.

The cornfields began to give way to houses. The small 'Welcome to Hilltop' sign appeared to his left. Ten minutes after passing it, he was turning onto what the townsfolk called Main Street. Bountiful Living was just a few blocks down.

Jonathan turned into the drive, the large black sign proclaiming, "We hope you enjoy your stay." He was pretty sure he wouldn't. There was a small parking lot and he found an empty spot under a tree.

It was nicer than he'd expected it to be. The grounds were landscaped and the walkways clean. The inside opened on a large gathering room. It was carpeted and had two chairs and a couch. There was also a television strategically positioned between the two. A large woman wearing a white lab coat was sitting behind a mahogany desk. A large white sign beneath it read, "Visitors must sign in."

Jonathan sat his box down and went over, picking up the clipboard in front of her.

"Who you here to see?"

Jonathan looked up. "Bailey Hazelwood."

"Are you Mr. Murray?"

"Yes, ma'am."

"Sign in there, someone will take you back."

Jonathan signed his name and sat down. The television was on but the sound was down. He'd begun daydreaming when a voice beckoned him.

"Mr. Murray?"

# KINGDOM

He turned around. "Yes?"

"You can go back now."

A large man in a white uniform was waiting. The man smiled but didn't speak. He led Jonathan down a brightly lit corridor. Doors lined it, some closed but most open. Inside he could see hospital beds, most occupied. There were a few others things, lamps and tables, but for the most part the rooms were bare. They turned left down another hallway and a woman burst from her room grabbing Jonathan's arm.

"Winston!" She shouted. "Oh come in, Winston. It's been so long."

Jonathan's first reaction was fear. "What?"

"Please, I'm just sitting down to dinner."

The orderly took her by the other hand. "Agnes, let's leave this poor boy alone."

"But it's my son!"

"No Agnes, he is here to see Mr. Hazelwood."

The old woman considered this, one hand going to her mouth. "Would you come back and visit me? I've been so lonely."

Unable to speak, Jonathan watched the orderly lead the woman back to her room.

"She just gets a little upset sometimes." He explained.

They walked down another hallway to another nurse's station. There were three women and an orderly standing behind it. When the other orderly saw Jonathan he shouted, "Hey Jimmy, that boy giving you trouble?"

"No, he's here to see Mr. Hazelwood."

"Well, he's in luck, I just took him breakfast so he hasn't had his meds' yet."

Jimmy nodded. "He's in room 309. Just go around that corner. You might want to knock before you go in."

Jonathan looked apprehensive. Jimmy smiled. "There won't be anymore jumping out at you. Most of these are too sick to get out of bed."

The number sat high on the door with perfect polished coldness. Jonathan could see the corner of a bed through the partially opened door. A man was sitting on the edge of it. There was a tray of food next to him and a window with a view of the courtyard. Jonathan pushed the door open, grateful that it didn't creak. Bailey heard the footsteps and turned.

"Yes?"

"Mr. Hazelwood."

At the sound of Jonathan's voice, the man stood up. "Did you bring my things?"

Jonathan held up the box.

Bailey nodded. "Bring it over."

Jonathan set the box on the bed. For a moment there was silence. It was Bailey who finally broke it.

"You want to sit down? I'm getting ready to eat this exquisite cuisine."

Jonathan found a chair and sat.

"You know, I'm not really sick enough to be in here. I had a case of pneumonia when I came in. I feel great, but they're not going to let me go home." It was half true.

"You don't have to stay long, I just wanted to thank you for going by and picking up these things for me."

"It's okay. I can stay for a little bit."

Bailey looked the boy over, decided something, then went back to eating. "You know, I understand why you were angry with me."

Jonathan looked at him. "I wanted to apologize for that."

Bailey took a bite of eggs, nodding.

"I was mad for a long time."

"Been hard since she left hasn't it?"

"Yeah, I compare every girl to her and can't find one who's good enough."

"She moved on though, didn't she?"

"Yeah, I guess she did."

"Well, they always do." The man sat his fork down and wiped his mouth. "Did you come here for the jars?"

The question caught Jonathan off guard. The man who'd asked it picked his fork back up and continued to eat his breakfast.

"No. I came to bring you your things," a pause, "and to apologize. I was an ass Mr. Hazelwood and I've wasted a friendship because of it."

"Here now, nobody said I wasn't your friend. It was you who quit coming around."

"I know, but you know what I mean."

"Time is a precious thing, Jonathan."

Jonathan waited for him to continue but he didn't. Instead, he went to the box and began unpacking it.

He took out a few things then set something aside.

"I want you to have this. It's not much, but it meant a lot to me once."

Jonathan tried to say no but Bailey wouldn't have it. He handed Jonathan the still life that once hung on his wall. There was no glass in front of it and the wooden frame was actual pieces of stick.

"I painted this a long time ago, one of the first ones I ever did. My mother made the frame for me."

"Why? I haven't spoken to you in years."

"When you get as old as I am, you forgive easily."

Jonathan took the picture from him. It felt alien in his hands.

"Take it home with you. You don't have to hang it up, just keep it. One day maybe you'll find a place for it."

Bailey stuck out his hand and Jonathan took it, shaking firm. "Now get on out of here before you waste anymore time, nothing in here but an old man coming to the end of the road."

"Would it be okay if I came to visit you? There's still a few stories left to tell, and your advice on things is always good."

"If you like, but on one condition."

"What?"

"Bring me some Corona Imperials."

# Chapter Sixteen

Jonathan graduated May the following year. School had been a burden for the most part and he was glad to see the preliminary portion of it behind him. He'd been to see Bailey numerous times during the past month and the old man enjoyed the visits more than he'd admit. The two talked mostly of girls and college, the war and the old days but it was a rainy afternoon in August when the topic of Emily came up.

"Why haven't you ever gone to see her?" Bailey asked, taking a puff of his cigar.

Jonathan leaned back in his chair and shrugged. "Hell, I don't know."

"Don't see why you don't take a trip to see her, close some of that off."

"She probably wouldn't remember me."

Bailey huffed, "She'd remember you."

Jonathan's mind filled with the old days, coming back as if they'd never left. He could see her standing on the sidewalk, hair dipped in the shadows of night. Maybe the old man was right, why not go see her? She'd sent his parent's an invitation to her graduation and his mother had returned with a card, congratulations, and twenty dollars. Jonathan had watched her put the return address into the drawer beside the telephone. He'd gotten it out and sat looking at the writing on the front. It was female, evident by the beauty of the lines, and written by her, evident by the hearts drawn over all the "i's".

Absence was a funny thing. When he was in her presence, she burned in everything he did. Once she was gone, his actions began to take on their own consequence. When enough time had passed he functioned without a thought of how she would think about something or what her opinion might be. Sitting there with Bailey, the realization of time and how little he had left came crashing in on him.

With high school over and college looming the fact was the address he had for her may not be good much longer. If she moved out of her parent's house, he would have difficulty finding her. He'd always held her in his head as stationary but realized now that the idea of her and where she was would soon be changing. If he was going to see her, he'd have to do it soon.

"Where'd you go?" Bailey asked.

Jonathan came back to the room. "Huh?"

"You checked out for a minute."

"I was just thinking."

"Thinking, huh?"

"Yeah."

"About her?"

"Yeah."

"You really should go see her. It would do you good."

"Yeah, I should shouldn't I?"

Bailey nodded. "Yes, and you should go now because its getting late and you'll need your rest for the long drive you're taking tomorrow."

"Tomorrow?"

"If you don't, you'll lose your nerve."

So by sunrise the next morning he was on the road. The ride was long but his spirits were high. He drove all day, his thoughts moving through memories, both painful and beautiful. It was everything welling up against a backdrop of the endless, winding landscape. He only stopped once to eat, and even then his mind never focused on anything but her, the prospect and the uncertainty. What he hoped to find was still a mystery to him, but it's what made it so wonderful, the not knowing.

It was seven in the evening when he saw exit seventy-four. As he came up to it, a sign for food and lodging directed him to the left. He pulled off. The neon green of the vacancy sign glowed in the humid evening. The lot wasn't too full so he pulled in and parked. The clerk was watching a television when Jonathan entered and she looked up.

"Good evening."

"Hey." Jonathan said. "How much for a single room?"

"Forty-two dollars if its just you."

"It's just me."

The room was on the second floor at the end of a short hallway and he used the key card to unlock the door. The interior was dark and smelled of uncirculated air. He flipped the light on revealing a small television and a single bed. The air conditioner was under the window and he pushed one of the buttons in. It began to wind up, blowing the thick curtains from side to side.

Exhaustion crowded every inch of his body but his mind was wide awake. He was within minutes of her house. It would be good to see her. A lot had happened between then and now. Perhaps the old feelings would give way to new ones. Maybe they could pick up where they left off. Part of him always believed they would be reunited. They'd fall back into love as easily as they'd done all those years ago. When he lay down, the darkness brought dreams of her.

When the sun broke, he felt an odd sense of fear. He struggled with the courage to get up and get moving and as the sleep wore away and reality drifted back in, he found he was hungrier than he was scared. He picked up the phone and ordered a small breakfast of eggs and bacon.

He sat eating, looking out the window at the

morning traffic passing by. To say that he wasn't nervous would be a lie, but the truth was he had to close this door. He'd left so much undone. He finished his breakfast, brushed his teeth and checked out.

He got back in the car and turned left, traveling five miles before turning on the first of a series of roads. Once leaving the main path, he wound through what could only be described as mountain country. After fifteen minutes of nothing, he came out on the other side and found himself in a very upscale part of town.

It was a beautiful place, the homes larger than any back home, all gilded with exquisite architecture and intense security. He'd never seen so many gates. After getting lost once he turned left onto a road called Partake Lane and found himself sitting at the entrance to her neighborhood. It was a gated community but apparently not during the day.

He rolled through, his tires leaving asphalt and crossing onto a small section of roadway made of brick. The lawns were pristine, clipped to the same height with greenness so intense they looked painted. He could tell the houses were old. It lent a certain charm to the elegance, though it did nothing for its unapproachable tone.

Her house, if the numbers he was passing were any indication, would be much further back. He was moving slow and he got a couple looks from angry old people. He sped up, trying to follow the numbers not to look suspicious.

Then it was there. He stopped at the bottom of the

drive and listened to his pounding heart. The reality came to him now, the size of the house, the distance in years. They'd been so young then, he realized she would probably be happy to see him, but that it would probably be a simple, "hey, how have you been" etc etc. The distance would hurt him but what could he do? He wasn't going to turn around.

He started to roll up the driveway but stopped when the front door came open and a young girl ran down the stairs. She went to a black BMW, grabbed something out of the backseat, and ran back inside. Just like that, her, in reality, the actual thing, moving before his eyes as she'd done so many years ago. It gave him the urgency he needed.

He rolled his car up the drive and stopped behind the car she'd just been in. With cobblestone under his feet, he took in the view. They were high on a hilltop overlooking the neighborhood. Then he was on the front steps, the doorbell a white glow. To touch it would set all into motion. He took a breath, held it, and reached out.

The circular light was cold beneath his fingers. When he pressed it, bells began ringing deep inside the house. They were followed by footsteps and a lock being thrown. When the door peeled back, Jonathan found himself staring at a face he recognized.

Whatever had made her beautiful as a girl had been accented as she grew. The blonde hair was cropped below her shoulders and seemed made of silk. She wasn't as tall as he was, but not much shorter. The curves of her body held perfect symmetry and for the first time in a long time he felt the strange winding up feeling in his head.

"Can I help ya?" The girl said, and though different he recognized the voice.

"Emily?" It came out nearly inaudible.

"Yes, do I know you?"

"You used to."

He watched as she took in his face and began trying to place it. It took a moment but as understanding dawned, he watched the put out face of a stranger melt into the accepting gaze of an old love. "Jonathan?"

Then it was his turn to smile. She came down the steps and wrapped her arms around him. She smelled of soft flowers, clean hair, and her. The swimming sensations were winding up and he made no attempt to stop them. Then her mouth was touching his. It was so unexpected he didn't know what to do. The old anger raced from his heart. She tasted like strawberries, an intoxicating mix of her perfume, lips, and memories. Jonathan found words trying to fly from his mouth but stilled them as to hold on to this as long as he could. Then, she pulled back and looked at him, looked at him as if he weren't real. "Do you want to come inside?"

The interior of the house yawned against him with its wood floors and dark hallways. She pulled him past a den where lush furniture accented an ancient stone fireplace, through a kitchen where an old Mexican woman was making bread, and to a large flight of stairs. She went up holding his hand. He kept trying to think of something to say but everything was moving so fast.

They moved down a hallway, past six doors and into her bedroom. It was bigger than two of his with high ceilings and long flowing curtains. The entire back wall was made of glass. The view was more amazing than the one he'd seen downstairs. A lake fell away towards the sky, lined on each side by towering green trees. Emily led him to a bed draped in silk and stood with her back to it staring at him.

"What in the world are you doing out here?"

"I came to see you."

"I thought you hated me."

"Maybe I did once."

"So you don't hate me anymore?"

He realized any hate he'd held for her was bred by his own selfishness. All he could do was shake his head.

"I thought about you a lot," she said, her eyes never leaving his, "after you hung up on me I was pretty pissed. Vowed never to speak to you again, but I got over it. I guess I understood. But you hurt me and I didn't forget that."

Jonathan started to say he was sorry but she wrapped her arms around him and pulled him backwards. He landed on top of her, feeling her legs open beneath him. "I think you owe me."

He wanted to kiss her, needed to kiss her, but he held off. "Owe you?"

She smiled then, and in her eyes he saw a sinister capacity of what she'd become dancing in their perfect blue clarity. "You and I have some unfinished business."

"I didn't come here for that." And he started to get up, but her hands tightened on his back. She smiled, eyes slanting until the color was gone. "Well, it's what you're going to get."

Prospects like this had come to his mind through the normal adolescent fantasies. He'd been with two girls in his life and loved neither, but they'd felt the same about him. Emily was always in his mind, everything based against what she was. Now, he found this prospect appealed to his animal instinct, but his heart was pulling him in another direction. He didn't want it to be like this, he didn't want her to be like this, but it was too late. Somewhere inside of him something very dark woke.

Then he was kissing her.

The need to have her was primal. They'd been lost to each other so long ago, now time had brought them home. Their mouths moved in simple precision, each one anticipating the move of the other in the way only purified lust can do. Her tongue moved into his mouth and he tasted her elixir. She could feel him hard against her and pushed her hips into him. When she reached for his belt he didn't waver, lifting himself enough so she could make easy work of it. Her fingers moved seamless.

"How long have you waited for this?" She whispered letting the softness of her breath fill his ear.

He didn't answer with words, but with his mouth and he felt her laugh to herself. It was a simple gesture laced with greed and venom. Then her hand opened his pants and snaked down towards the thing which waited for her. She encircled it, feeling its thickness, and began to stroke. The sensation drove him mad. He grabbed the edges of her shirt and pulled it over her head. She wore no bra and her breasts lay beautiful against her tanned skin.

For a moment he was paralyzed, caught in her grip like an insect. Then she released him and pulled his shirt off. He followed her lead and pulled the jogging pants she was wearing off. She wore no panties, and the naked mound glistened as she opened her legs.

It only took a moment for him to remove his pants. She guided him in, her eyes never leaving his. Then they were moving, the first entrance across oceans of time. They clawed and ground against each other, heat and flesh mixing with sweat and semen and no sound but their breathing, the uncontrolled moans and the cries that finally brought them to climax.

Beyond the room, the sky had begun to darken. She could feel the wetness around Jonathan who still lay within her and could feel his thickness softening. He slipped himself out of her and lay next to her breathing.

"Not bad." She said and reached across him for a pack of cigarettes. "Didn't think I'd ever get to do that."

"You could have called and asked me to come down."

"No, I was waiting for you. I told myself if you ever came, I was going to have you in me."

Jonathan didn't recognize the girl lying next to

him. Hadn't recognized her since he'd come to the house. It was no doubt that she was Emily, but it was some other form of Emily.

"So do you have a girlfriend?"

"No." Jonathan said.

"I have a fiancée', how's that one for you."

The slap to his heart was unexpected but not unfamiliar. "Fiancée?"

"Yeah, his name's Brandon. I met him a year ago at a party. He's a pretty cool guy, drinks too much though, likes to sleep with my friends, but other than that." She took a drag on her cigarette.

Jonathan felt out of place and wrong. "So what are we doing?"

"Us? We were fucking. What did you think we were doing?"

Jonathan didn't answer. A sensation of surrealism was beginning to build up.

"I mean don't get me wrong, I like you a lot, used to love you, but it's been a long time you know? Don't look so shocked, I thought that's what you came up here for."

"I just wanted to see you, tell you I was sorry for all that back then. I wasn't just coming here to have sex with you."

Emily smiled and took another drag. "Well, I'm glad you did."

Jonathan's mind was caught in the illusion of putting two people over one memory. The girl before him was Emily, but it wasn't the Emily he'd known. "You're a lot different then I thought you'd be."

"Yeah, chalk it up to experience."

"I should probably go."

"Relax, I'm picking on you. There's nowhere for you to go anyway. The ride back to your place will be too long. Just go to sleep, you can leave tomorrow."

On the lake outside, small red and blue lights crossed to and fro. It didn't take long for Emily's breathing to change and for Jonathan to realize she was asleep. A vivid memory rushed back, one that smelled of summer and old wood. The two of them holding each other while rain tapped an ancient rooftop.

He got out of the bed then not wanting to face the reality before him, and walked around the bedroom. There were pictures of her and her friends, pictures of places and people he'd never seen. A lifetime of faces and memories and all as alien to his as she was. In a drawer beside her bed he found an array of old papers and clothes, beneath these he found something he recognized.

He hadn't seen its in years, had assumed it lost to some far ago time or packed with care in some forgotten box, yet there it was, the face he'd remembered, the way he'd drawn it, the way that his heart had seen her, every imperfection, every perfect line, staring back at him again. It was the way he felt when he looked at pictures of Arielle, nothing but the reflection of light from a thing that had once had the capacity to reflect it, but Jonathan knew that light was only part of it. The truth lay not only in the light, but in the dark behind the light.

Somewhere along the line, she'd changed. Probably

by things she couldn't control. Maybe by what he'd done to her, cutting her off with his selfishness. It was too far gone to change and too hurtful to think about. How different could things have been if he'd only been a friend to her? He didn't know. He climbed back in beside her and felt her roll against him. She snuggled in, sleep erasing all the walls she'd held up earlier. He could see glimpses of her and it was these he held to as he went into the dark.

In the morning he woke alone, shirtless and freezing. The door was open and he could hear someone walking around downstairs. The footsteps were soon accompanied by voices, two by the sound, and as he bent to put on his shoes Emily came up the stairs with another girl.

"Cute." The new one said, taking in Jonathan.

"Isn't he? Jonathan, I want you to meet Megan. Megan is one of my best friends."

"One of?" The girl said faking irritation.

"Fine, she's my one and only."

"That's better."

The girls laughed, their gaze never leaving him. Megan continued to look at him.

"How are you?" He asked continuing to tie his shoes.

"Good now."

Emily left the girl standing in the doorway and sat down on the bed next to him. "You leaving?"

"I have to get back." There was awkwardness to his voice he didn't like.

"What do you think of Megan?"

Jonathan didn't look up. "Seems nice."

"No silly, what do you think of her?"

The girl wasn't as pretty as Emily but it was a close race. He began to understand the situation for what it was and knew if he didn't get out of here things might get out of control.

"The thing with me and Megan is, whatever we like we share, clothes, boys, whatever. She'd like to try you Jonathan, if you have time. I've been singing your praises."

"Don't you think that's a little weird?"

"Oh come on, what guy wouldn't want to? If it'll make you feel better, I'll hold your hand."

Emily made a gesture towards Megan and the girl crossed to the other side of him. Again the sensation of surrealism began filling his head.

"We're going off to college in the fall. After that, I probably won't see you much. I'd just like to leave you with something to remember."

"You already have," he said speaking more of their early years than the night before.

Then there were fingers in his hair. He could smell both girls and felt himself growing to the occasion.

"Just this once." Emily purred.

Megan began kissing his neck. The sensation was riveting and it took all his will to keep from giving in to it.

"Please, Jonathan." She said, and the sound of her speaking his name drove the horde of emotions away.

Hands were reaching under his shirt, the soft

warmth of flesh stroking his chest. They were laughing, reaching, pushing him back. Jonathan found himself remembering her as she was, the girl he'd fallen in love with, and with the thought came ones of unfamiliarity, ones laced in confusion.

He pushed them off and stood up. Megan gave Emily a puzzled glance and lay back on the bed.

"You can't leave until I say!" Emily screamed. He went out the door with her at his heels, each word a dagger intending to wound, but he was beyond their reach. When he reached the stairs a sound made him stop. Emily was crying.

She stood behind him, desperation in her eyes. "Please, don't go."

He wondered how so many layers could exist in one soul. "I can't stay if you're like this."

"Like what?"

"Like this."

"This is how I am now, I'm not trying to hurt you."

"You can't act like this with me. I didn't come up here for this."

Her gaze never left his. "I still love you Jonathan and I didn't forget you."

He could only stare at her. "I never forgot you either."

"Then stay, I can make Megan leave, you and me can hang out."

"I have to go."

"Why?"

"I just can't be here like this."

She stood and ran her hand down his face. He could see the tears again but she held them. Whatever it was she had become, it was in response to survival. Her innocence would have been considered weakness.

She stared at him with a face too beautiful to bring its owner anything but pain and sighed.

"Would it be okay if I came to see you before I leave for college?"

"Yeah, that'd be nice. Mom and dad would get a kick out of seeing you."

"You think they'd remember me?"

"You're not easily forgotten."

Emily put her hand in his. "I'll give you a call before I come." She squeezed, the sensation bringing back old emotions, then kissed his cheek. "Be careful, it's a long drive."

He turned from her, somehow sure that he would never see her again and opened the door. He could hear the sounds of the people moving around in the kitchen. Pans were banging and plates were being put away. All around him was movement. Even before he left the foyer, the house had fallen back into its rhythm.

The potency of love and memory was a fragile thing and Jonathan knew, as he'd known so many years before, that in his absence the old numbness would return and things would naturally move back to the way they had been before he came. It was a prospect that no longer surprised him. He was fully aware of what it meant to be surrounded by people who looked at you as you looked at them, pieces of a life once lived.

# KINGDOM

The interstate was a time of reflection. The scenery was nothing more than a canvas for his mind to paint on. Hours later, when he crossed into Morning Ridge, the familiar sense of home stole over him. Yet across each street, he saw it was no longer home to him. Little pieces of what he'd held so dear had been scattered to the wind. Emily, Arielle, Mr. Hazelwood, the town, and it would only get worse. It scared him to begin again. To start a new life with someone, because the constant change would not stop. Each day brought everything further from where it was the day before. If the moments could be captured, it would be a paradise, a utopia of existence, and he felt goose flesh stand up on his arms.

# Chapter Seventeen

Jonathan was trying to figure out how to work the microwave when the mail arrived. There were a few bills and a letter proclaiming, "you've been pre-approved". Behind it was one he didn't like the look of. The envelope was from Bountiful Living and the writing on the front was Bailey's.

In February, Bailey had suffered a stroke leaving the right side of his body paralyzed. It had done something to his mind as well and their visits became less frequent. The old man wanted to be by himself and Jonathan hadn't pressed the issue. That had been three weeks ago.

# KINGDOM

Mr. Hazelwood had been on his mind a lot lately and it made the letter feel heavy in his hands. The sight of his name in Bailey's unmistakable script made him wonder when the letter had been written. He set the rest of the mail on the table and went to the porch where the light was better. With a shaking finger he ran it along the inside of the flap. Inside was a folded piece of paper. Jonathan took it out and opened it.

The date at the top fueled his fears, it was three months previous. It would have been colder then, snowing. The image of Mr. Hazelwood bent over his desk while white drifts floated past the courtyard window filled Jonathan with loneliness so hard it made his chest hurt.

Below the date was a greeting, "Dear Jonathan," a formal letter. Then, as he began to read, he found himself lost.

"Dear Jonathan, I don't mean to be melodramatic but if you're reading this then one of two things has happened. That sweet chariot has carried me to the land by and by or I've become immobilized to the point I will never be remobilized. I pray for the first but know the second is as likely as the other. In any event, I made a promise to you a long time ago. I'm sure that you remember. There was a time when I thought I wouldn't see you grow to be the man you should be, one with compassion and understanding of the world. I know that you still have much to learn, but over time, especially recently, I've seen a change in you. That angry boy has grown into a young man that looks at things before diving into them. I've also found a good friend in you. You've helped to brighten an old man's days and for that, I'll be forever grateful. So I decided today after you brought me the hot soup and sandwich, do you remember what day I'm talking about?"

Jonathan did. It had been the coldest day of his life with the wind chill in the negative and a layer of snow that came to his knees. His mother had fixed vegetable soup for dinner, setting aside an extra container for Mr. Hazelwood.

The following morning he'd scraped the windows on his father's truck and set off. He made one stop before heading towards Bountiful Living. It was a deli on the corner of Fifth and Rose which made 'one hell of a' roast beef on rye.

When he arrived at Bailey's bedside the man looked worn down, but when he saw the food Jonathan had his eyes perked up. He tore into the sandwich and once it was gone he looked more like himself.

They'd talked for hours and when the sun started to set Jonathan realized the weather was too bad to leave. With permission from the home, he spent the night. The two continued their conversation well into the evening.

The note in his hand started to blur. Jonathan concentrated and continued.

"In any event, I told you a story a long time ago about a young boy and his first love and the loss he sustained because of it. I was never able to understand or control what Camille gave to me. I'm not sure if she was leaving me a way to find her or not. I tried,

God how I tried, but I only ended up purging myself of goodness. I turn over to you what I was not able to solve. It is your choice how you proceed. You're a smart boy Jonathan. Do you remember the picture I gave you?"

He thought of the still life hanging on his bedroom window.

"Finish it and you'll find what you're looking for. Don't get too down if you find I'm gone. It's been a good life for me. Good luck son, you're probably going to need it." With that the old man signed his name.

Jonathan refolded the paper and stuck it in his pocket. For a long time he only sat there staring at the 'for sale' sign in Bailey's front yard. The summer had come again, so many summers behind and many left to be and he felt old. At eighteen he felt used up. The old world was pulling away one string at a time. What once was strong now stretched before him frayed and uncertain.

He went inside and called Bountiful Living. His old pal Jimmy answered and recognized Jonathan's voice. When he did, the man's tone changed and Jonathan knew without having to ask.

"Was it quick?"

"Went in his sleep day before yesterday. Made me promise to send you that letter if anything were to happen to him. You got it right?"

"Yeah. What about a funeral?"

"Wanted to be cremated. I suppose they'll keep the ashes there until someone claims him. Not real sure how it'll work."

"Well, he really liked you." Jonathan said.

"Yeah, we're gonna miss him around here. You take care."

Jonathan hung up the phone.

The picture hung above the lamp on his dresser. He pulled it off the wall and began looking it over. He wound his hands around every inch trying to uncover something. He turned it over and looked at the back. He laid it on the bed and pulled the note out again, fearing he'd missed something.

It was a simple enough picture, a table, or maybe a shelf, walled on two sides with containers jutting into the shadows. There was a scrap of napkin, or paper, he couldn't tell which and what looked like an orange. The focal point was an old rusted can with the letters "AI" visible on it. Finish it? What did it mean?

Again he ran his fingers along the edge, tilting it sideways as he did. The motion of his hand brushed against something small and he pulled it back expecting a splinter. What he saw was a black smudge. He rubbed it against his palm recognizing the texture at once. Feeling around the edges he found the source of this unexpected discovery. A quick snap against his palm brought a single sliver of charcoal loose from it's crevice. It fell onto his bed and rolled down a fold in the blanket. When it did, something clicked in his mind. When he held it up to the light he saw metallic specs glistening within it.

His eyes were scanning. The picture looked completed to him, every inch of it filled with some pigment of color or shade. Back and forth he went,

# KINGDOM

trying to move along with skilled precision. After three tries he became discouraged. It was finished, no white space anywhere, nothing out of place.

Then the paint can caught his attention. The entire word was spelled out across it if you looked close, PAINT. The AI portion of it was small, but they were clear. The other letters were not. Pulling the picture as close as he dared he was able to see bare canvas shining through. Except that wasn't quite right, it was bare but had be written upon once. The faint highlights of eraser marks were evident in the hard light beside his bed.

A sensation began, one which came from a place much deeper than his wakeful mind. It saw what it needed to do and hungered for the chance to do it. With a steady hand he put the picture down and brought the charcoal up. The empty space was huge in his mind's eye, the size of a mountain. His hand moved with a surgeon's skill, pulling down and across, scraping off small pieces of the metallic resin.

As if in a trance, his fingers began their work. The interior of his nail ran around the edging bringing out the excess. A hard blow and it puffed up around him. He took the note from his back pocket meaning to have Bailey as close to him as he could. He tore off a small scrap and rolled it tightly between his fingers. The tip was as sharp as a nail and he dipped it down, shading the letters to match the hue of the ones which already lay there. As he finished, he took the back of his thumb and ran it first across, then up, blending the lines. The unmistakable purged feeling began to show around the corners of his mind. He was coming back from the subconscious halls. The real world began to fade back in, the picture in his hands becoming part of it.

With his head clear he sat staring. He wasn't sure what to expect so after twenty minutes of nothing he began to feel like he'd done something wrong. Maybe the shade was too dark, maybe he'd missed something else, yet there was no way it could have been. To the untrained eye those letters were never white. Still, he reached down to brush at one of the metal pieces hoping to clear away a portion of dust that was hiding something and when he did his hand passed through what would have been the plain of canvas into the darkness beyond. He knocked something metal off its perch and clanged it onto its side. He recoiled in surprise and nearly fell off the bed.

He could hear the sound of his parents moving around downstairs, could hear the soft murmur of the television. All his senses were on high alert warning him of the impossibility of what he'd just experienced, warning him, as Mr. Hazelwood would have warned him, to be careful.

He moved towards the painting, a hole framed by fragile wood, and hesitated as his fingers dipped into the dark. The air inside was heavy but cool. The unmistakable scent of age wafted up as he moved his arm deeper, disappearing into what should have been his mattress.

What was once a painting was now a window, the image it had been was still there, somehow hanging untouched by gravity. There was a scrap of linen within his reach and he plucked it up. He brought it out slow, careful not to catch it on the edge of the frame. With it in his hands he saw something he didn't expect, Bailey's handwriting.

There was a clarity here that his later writing lacked. The lines were crisper, the dots surer. It looked like a recipe. He held it closer to the light marveling at the insanity of the patterns. There were phrases and partial sentences. "Remember, the inside reflects partial..." and "Fourteen better than nine..." In both margins, calculations based off strange symbols ran up one side and down the other. On the back the patterns continued, small drawings of circles and arcs, random numbers and portions that had been scribbled out. If there was meaning here, it wouldn't be easy to uncover.

Setting the paper aside he peered back into the dark and saw something reflecting light. Still cautious, but less hesitant, he let his fingers drift through darkness until they touched something made of glass. He felt his heart racing and felt fresh lunatic possibility spring up in his head.

The jar came into the room throwing a million points of reflection as tiny specs of metallic dust caught the light. His hands were trembling but he found himself unable to avert his eyes. Here was the promise kept. He brought it closer, his thumb stroking the ancient dirty glass. He could see other things in the jar as well. Mixed with the metallic specs were two shades of powder, one yellow, one ash grey.

# JEREMY RANDOLPH

They ran in patterns, mixed but separated and a fresh memory came to him, one of Arielle's skin and the veins beneath it. Part yet separate.

The next thing out was a wooden cup, its edges worn and busted. Inside were seven brushes covered in dust with hair slipping out from the main bristles like web. Jonathan touched the tops of these loving the clatter of wood as they moved against each other. "These were the ones he used," he thought.

After the brushes came a jar of charcoal sticks. They were pattern makers, the edging tools. Unlike the powder jar, this one had no lid. He ran his fingers across the tops and felt an electric, almost painful sensation dance across his skin. He held his fingers up and saw the black smudges mingled with the same metallic resin. At first he'd associated it with glitter, but close up he saw they were metal shavings.

The final two items to be removed didn't seem to have much importance; one was an empty paint can, the other an orange. With everything out he could bring he sat back with the paper and began looking it over. After an hour, he brought out his own paper and began making notes, hoping to translate some of the lunacy that ran rampant throughout the wording. It was apparent the writings would make sense to Bailey, but to him they were just snippets of thoughts and calculations. There was even a phone number, which he called, and found disconnected. He skipped dinner and watched the sun go down still no closer to an answer.

The obvious assumption was that you took a

picture, drew it, and somehow created a window into the picture. It seemed simple enough, but there was the powder, and according to the notes a process of mixture which was either coded or left out all together. There was also the question of closing the painting back up. You could draw a picture and open it but how did you close it again? The painting had some of its white space removed, but how did you make it solid so that you could remove the white space? Questions without answers he supposed were better than no questions at all. He fell asleep around three in the morning, the paper on his chest, jars sitting silent on his nightstand.

When he woke the painting still yawned open on the bed beside him. It wasn't a dream, all reality. He went to the jars and brought them over. There was an issue of secrecy he needed to take care of. He couldn't leave the jars sitting around, it would open them to the prospect of discovery. He formulated a plan, though course of action was probably a better term, and didn't want to leave anything out in the open.

The picture was the obvious place. He'd put them back and worry about getting it closed again once he got some breakfast. One by one he set the jars inside then headed downstairs.

Both parents roamed the town on Sunday's running errands so he was alone. A quick inspection of the fridge revealed nothing to eat without having to cook so he poured himself a glass of orange juice and popped two pastries in the toaster. While he waited, he looked around the kitchen. Though colorful in the light of morning, there was a grayness hanging on the edges. Behind him the toaster popped. He dropped his pastries on a plate and went back up to his room.

The picture was where he'd left it and still just as open as before. The thought occurred to him that he may not be able to figure out how to close it. He finished his pastries and set the plate aside, took a final mouthful of orange juice and reached for the painting. As he brought it forward the ancient air puffed into his face and he felt a sneeze start to build. He tried to swallow the mouthful of juice, and almost succeeded but the sneeze came with enough spray to get his arms and pants wet. The picture got a good coat of it too and he cursed himself for being so careless.

He pulled his T-shirt off and began wiping the frame with it. At first it was hard because of the intricacies but as he passed the shirt from one edge to the other he noticed a peculiar thing. The shirt didn't pass into the picture, at least not where the sprays of juice had connected with it. He tested this theory and found that where he'd wiped juice there was solidity. There was still a little residue in his glass and he turned it upside down onto the corner of his shirt. He moved the shirt towards the painting, to a place where there was no solidity, and was dumbfounded when the shirt passed through into the dark. He sat for a moment, not sure what he was missing, then the light blinked on.

It only took a second to get another glass of juice. He took a small bit in his mouth and hesitated. Spitting orange juice onto something so important seemed

# KINGDOM

ludicrous but it was the only thing that made sense. The first burst hit the frame and began to run down. When it got to the point where the canvass would be it did not drip in, but slid down. Jonathan reached out with his finger and began rubbing the small tear of juice and found that as he spread, it solidified. He pulled his notepad over and wrote.

"Oranges are the key to closing the picture. Not sure if it's the acid or some other chemical, but the juice (compound) must be applied through the air. You cannot wipe it until it's touched it. Here is what I am calling Theory One: The Subject of Solidity.

All particles on the earth are made up of atoms, protons, neutrons, the whole thing. Dependant upon their chemical composition, temperature, etc they are solids, liquids, or gasses. Ice is just water until it melts, and then you can swim in it; drown in it, bath in it. The picture is like that, when you first paint it you create its form, you create it, something from nothing. Then its makeup is existent. Now, it appears that the default makeup of this creation is always either a gas or in our example, water, so a liquid, something you can pass through. For whatever reason, when you place liquid orange juice onto this compound you change the makeup of it at a chemical level and, while it's still the same thing (aka water) it turns to a solid (aka ice) thus the orange juice acts like the temperature agent. This process is repeatable and reversible as long as the creative object is constructed following specific rules which I have yet to determine."

With it written down he ran juice upon the picture

until it was once again solid. Then, picking up the pad again he wrote:

"Not sure if the items behind the picture are also changed in solidity or if the initial layer has some reflective capabilities that allows it to hold the last bit of light (like a camera lens) that passed through it. It is apparent that the field, and or the creation is transparent in nature, thus I cannot prove or disprove the behind"

He spent the rest of the day making more notes, coming up with ideas and hypothesis. The similarities to Arielle and her notebooks never occurred to him, but was it so strange that he adopted some of her behaviors? If he were to dwell on this topic he might find the same patterns he was finding in his notes on "Composition of Jars A-B". The assimilation of her traits, as he was her brother, like her, part of her, as she would be part of him.

For three days he worked, mindless of anything but the observations and limitation he was facing at his current locale. The research, as he was now referring to it, would have to be continued somewhere else. The next morning he packed up some supplies and made his way back to a place he'd not been in over six years. It had been in disarray the last time he'd seen it, but it was the perfect place to go for what he was intending to do.

When he ascended the creek and crossed through the overgrowth he was surprised to see their place still standing. In fact, it looked as though someone had repaired it. The windows, broken before, were now replaced. The walls seemed firmer and there was a fresh coat of either paint or stain, from his vantage he couldn't be sure. However, the mystery was quickly solved as he approached. The property had been sold. Remnants of an old "For Sale" sign leaned against the wall. New owners meant new possibilities and with that came an idea.

He walked up at the main house, a place he'd never actually been in all his years of trespassing and rang the doorbell. When he was a boy, Conrad Morris and his family had owned the property. When the door opened this time it was a much younger man. The new owner, a man named Ralph Baker, had no issue or need for the building. He'd bought the property as a development opportunity but was caught up in litigation over its "historical value". Gaining some monetary value, however small, would be just fine with him. He collected the first months rent, saying a hundred dollars would be enough for a disheveled old shack, gave Jonathan the keys to the newly installed doors, and excused himself back to his breakfast.

The terms were, he could come and go as he pleased. Jonathan had expressed his need for privacy, was granted permission of privacy, and if Mr. Baker needed to contact him he would call his parents house. Thus the deal was set, money exchanged, and Jonathan became the proud renter of a place he'd always considered his. He considered the turn of events and felt even stronger about his intentions.

By dusk, he was beneath the soft glow of the interior light supplied by a small generator stolen from his father's shed. Before him were blank pieces of paper. For most of the night he would sketch on these, using the part of his mind not controlled by his gift to do the initial planning phase. When he'd gotten everything he thought he needed, he packed up his remaining supplies, locked the door, and made his way through the dark towards home, the old place watching him as its true occupant made his way home.

# Chapter Eighteen

Three weeks passed. The first of these was what he considered the "preparation phase". He'd gone to the local shops to pick up supplies, a small desk, paper, etc., and carried them out to their place. It was slow going but it gave him time to theorize. It was what he was calling the second week, the "theorize phase." He'd not given much thought to what he would call the third week until she called. He now considered it "the path of uncertainty." The phone rang at eleven o' two and he recognized the voice on the other end immediately. Emily sounded like she'd been running. Between pants she managed to get out, "How are you?" Jonathan had told her fine, he was a hell of a lot more than fine, but why bother saying, and went on fixing his breakfast. It turned out she hadn't been running but packing. She and her friend, presumably Megan, were going up to the university to look for an apartment. Why she would pack before going was a mystery to him, but he had bigger things to worry about. There was no mention of the events that had occurred between them. Emily rode through the conversation on auto pilot. It took Jonathan awhile to understand everything she was saying but when her breathing finally evened out he was able to follow without much trouble.

The fiancée she'd had was now another broken heart. The prospect of college was more powerful than the prospect of settling down and Emily had dropped him as she dropped everything when it didn't fit her plan. He supposed he loved that about her once, that unrelenting refusal of conformity. Still, the reason for the call eluded him. It was as though she'd gotten a wild hair and thought it'd be fun to call him.

"So what are you doing today?"

It was the first direct thing she'd asked him. The rest had all been a babble of information with him saying, "uh huh", and "yeah."

"Not much, probably just hang around here. I have some stuff I need to take care of."

"Sounds exciting."

"I guess so."

A pause. "What are you doing this weekend?"

"Not sure, why."

"I was thinking about coming down to see you."
"See me? Why?"
"Well, I told you I would."
"Oh, yeah."
"Forgot already huh, well, I'd like to see you anyway, but if you don't want me too, I won't."
"No, it's fine if you want too, it's just a long way to come."
"Don't get too excited."
Jonathan didn't reply.
"Well it'd be on Friday. Since I'll already be out from home I figured I'd make a week of it. Find an apartment, come see an old friend. Do you think your parents would mind?"
"Probably not, I could let you sleep in my room, but I'd have to stay on the couch, we don't have an extra room." It was a lie in concrete but true in emotion. They did have Arielle's room but it hadn't been slept in since she'd died.
"That's fine. You can sneak up when they're asleep." She giggled then, a sound that reminded him of the girl she used to be. "So is it a date?"
"I wouldn't call it a date, but it would be good to see you again. Maybe we could talk this time."
"Yeah, didn't get a lot of that done last time did we?"
There was an odd sensation of silence and undercurrent and it too him a moment to speak. "No."
"Okay then, well look for me sometime around eight or so."

"I will."
"Keep dinner warm."
"What?"
"Just kidding. I'll see you then."

Jonathan hung up the phone. Sometimes he felt trapped. Every time he thought he found his bearings another change would send him reeling. So she wanted to come see him now? What the hell was that about, and why now? It didn't matter in any event, he had work to do. He finished the rest of his breakfast and headed out.

The door leading to his new abode was a huge wooden thing with a dead bolt and ancient latch. The key slipped nimbly into the shiny brass lock and it took two turns to dispel the bolt. He put the key back in his pocket and turned the knob. He'd boarded up the windows so the initial entrance was total darkness and his immediate thought was, "looks like a tomb," which wasn't totally untrue. No light and no real source of air circulation made it unpleasant at times. He'd brought a fan from home but it didn't do much except blow the warm air around.

The bulk of his sketches were preliminaries, but as with all his drawings, they were exquisite. Beneath these were unlined sheets of drawing paper. He extracted a few and sat down in the floor.

He picked out two pieces of charcoal and set them beside the paper. He was planning on drawing a patch of grass, nothing special, just a few blades, but it would be his first experiment of the day. He picked up the charcoal and was again amazed at its weight. When his eyes went to the paper, he saw the image trying to emerge in his mind. The sensation was followed by the winding up one.

It didn't take long to finish. He reached out, expecting to pass through the picture and touch the grass beyond, but did not. His hands hit the cold wooden floor. Wincing a little he tried to figure out what he'd done wrong. All the white space was gone, nothing remained but the grass and the sky beyond. It was in all aspects finished. Bailey's note had been specific on that point.

"There can be no portion of incompleteness. One must fully create the place one sees."

The rain was beginning to come down harder. He could hear it slapping the roof. He'd been stuck on this portion for nine days. What had he done wrong? Restless, he got a fresh sheet and started again. The more he drew the more hopeless it all seemed. Picture after picture bringing nothing but frustration and he was running out of things to draw. There were only so many birds and trees he could draw before he had to open the door and draw an actual thing.

He scanned the room and found a candy wrapper lying upside down in the corner. He decided to sketch it out then call it a day, he was getting hungry and the rain wasn't slowing. It didn't take long before a photographic likeness of the wrapper stared back at him. He sat the charcoal aside and stretched. When he did he thought he saw movement in the picture. It was probably lack of sleep but he moved his hand towards it just the same.

# JEREMY RANDOLPH

There was a moment when he thought the same thing was going to happen again. He would hit the floor and curse his stupidity. His hand developed a noticeable shake as it descended towards the picture. The constant rattle of the generator rose above the cascading rain. Where there should have been floor, his hand passed through the black layers of charcoal and what he touched wasn't hardwood but a crinkled candy wrapper.

He brought it out and held it to his nose. The smell of chocolate resonated. He knew if he went to the wall and retrieved the real one, the same scent would greet his nose only that wasn't the case. The one in the corner was gone. Keeping his eye on that location he dipped the wrapper back through. To his amazement, his fingers appeared on the other side of the room.

He dropped the wrapper and pulled his hand back. There were now two bars, one in the picture and one against the far corner wall. He hadn't created a new scene he'd opened a window. With whatever gift he held and through whatever magic was in the charcoal, he'd managed to cut a piece of reality free from its molding. Now the rest of the pictures made sense. Of course they hadn't opened, they had never existed. They was a product of his imagination.

"Be careful, Jonathan." It was Mr. Hazelwood's voice from some long ago afternoon.

And he intended to be.

It took an hour to complete his final test. When the picture opened, it opened into his father's tool shed. What he brought out wasn't candy but a small wooden car, one he'd made in the scouts long before he'd lost interest in the communities of boydom. It would be the final piece, proof that his intentions were not unfounded. It was a perfect piece of molded wood. The paint still shone with its uncertain hues, the way his father had helped him, the way Jonathan had let him, knowing full well that the pallet was not condusive to art. Yet this particular piece of wood, this care that now felt so heavy in his hands, had been crushed beneath the wheels of his father's truck eleven years before. With shaking hands, he clutched its familiar shape and stared out the open door into the rushing downpour of water.

# Chapter Nineteen

As his plans increased, blooming like a flower in spring, he'd become increasingly nervous about leaving his things at their place. When he first started coming he'd leave the charcoal and paper, comforted by the deadbolt and the no trespassing sign. Now, he left nothing.

The things he was doing in the small four walled room had begun to have an effect on his mind. Never one for paranoia, he found he needed to come out at least twice a day to check on their place. He'd begun taking alternate routes, going around behind houses and cross the creek at different locations to keep the possibility of someone following him down. He'd also begun to suspect his parents were growing suspicious and he began acting even stranger around them, avoiding them if he could. Then he became convinced Mr. Baker might have a spare set of keys and that he'd come in, see what Jonathan was doing, and then what? He didn't want to know. He'd changed all the locks and added a few more for good measure and even though it took longer to get inside, it was well worth it. He'd constructed an elaborate method of strings and positioning so he would know if anyone had come in while he was away and still the constant nagging to check would not leave him. He took a look around, saw nothing was out of place, and closed the door.

Emily had called that morning to verify her arrival. Jonathan hadn't been home but his mother said Emily expected to get there around seven, an hour earlier than she'd told him the previous weekend. When she pulled into the driveway, he was waiting, sitting on the porch. She didn't get out right away so he went to see if she needed help unloading. He'd thought, quite stupidly he'd thought, that he wouldn't be affected by her presence. When she looked at him, averting her eyes from the visor mirror, he felt a rush he hadn't expected. She smiled, accenting the things that made her far too beautiful, and looked back at the mirror. "Come to walk me in?"

"Something like that."

She wiped her lips and snapped the visor up. "Well I didn't bring anything you need to carry. I'm not moving in you know." She winked and climbed out.

Jonathan watched her come around the side of the car, the sun dancing off her tanned skin, and thought again how unprepared he was for her. The need to love her welled but he couldn't decide if it was a true emotion or not. The breasts and curves of her hips called to the primal urges in him, yet overlapping these was that sense of lost friendship, time spent learning one another. With her as she was he had an "in" of sorts, but the uncertainty of her as she was now lent an uncertainty to her. It was the balance of light and dark, contrast and shading, all spinning, all encompassing.

"You shouldn't look at me like that out here in the open, people might start talking." She touched his fingers and walked up onto the porch.

"Are you hungry?" He asked.

"No I got something to eat on the way. I am sorta thirsty though."

Jonathan took her to the kitchen and brought out a jug of lemonade. It had been years since Emily had been there and she marveled at how familiar it felt. The house brought back memories that were as unexpected as the feelings Jonathan had endured upon her arrival. There was a sense of guilt returning to a place left undone and that had been how she'd left it, undone. The things inside had been touched by times hand, the faded curtains, the yellowing tile, yet their original brilliance was still evident beneath the wearing of age and it conjured emotions she didn't want to feel.

They sat at the table drinking lemonade and trying to make small talk. Her gaze never left him. It was a powerful thing and in it there was no balance, she had the upper hand.

"So you came down to visit me?" Jonathan asked.

"Yeah, you seem a little freaked out about it though."

"No, not really, I've just got a lot on my mind."

"A lot on your mind huh? Big things going on in Morning Ridge, is the church having a bake sale?"

The comment wasn't meant to hurt him but it brought an effect of belittlement just the same. "No, nothing as exciting as that, I just have things on my mind."

"You always did, didn't you?" The comment was one of remembrance and he accepted it as such.

"I suppose." He took a drink and fiddled with his cup. "How long are you staying for?"

"I haven't decided yet. I'll let you know."

"You do that."

"I will."

"So when does college start?"

"In the fall."

"You're not making this easy." He said.

"No, but you're making it fun," and she winked at him.

"Mom and Dad said you could sleep in my room tonight."

"What makes you think I want to sleep with you in your room?"

"I just assumed."

"You know I'm teasing you."

Once the lights were out and the stillness of night set in, Emily didn't sleep in much. A white tee shirt and panties served as her attire. Jonathan lay shirtless on the floor staring at the ceiling, the patterns doing their constant swirl. He marveled at the fact she was here and wondered again why he'd been so stupid to let her get so distant. The girl in the bed was just a shadow of Emily, but he still remembered how she was. She would always be that girl to him, the pure, funny, totally unafraid girl who'd laughed and kissed him in a place that seemed like a dream to him now. He could hear her soft breathing and he felt a crush of loneliness steal over him so deep that he had to steady himself to breathe. Left behind, that's what he felt. She'd gone off and changed and he'd been left behind. There was no way to catch up with her, no way to redo those days that had slipped by.

"Are you okay down there?" Her voice, yet not her.

"Yeah."

"You sleeping?"

"No."

"Feel like talking?"

He felt like screaming. "Sure."

"I wanted to come down here cause we left things kinda messed up."

"It's no big deal."

"Well yeah, it kinda is. You did something to me up there."

"Yeah, I know."

"I'm not talking about the sex."

"Oh."

"That thing with Megan, I've never seen a guy turn her down. Usually we use guys up, throw them out and laugh about it."

"I really don't want to hear about this," and he didn't. An odd sick feeling had gripped his stomach. It felt like his balls were trying rise up through his throat.

"It's okay."

And like hell it was but he shut up.

"Anyway, after that I had a different opinion of guys. They were good for playing with, getting money from and using for my own personal entertainment. There were plenty to do it with, so that's what life became. Self pleasure, everything and as much as I could take."

He heard the mattress creak as she sat up. "God, you wouldn't believe some of the shit I did. I was the popular girl, everybody wanted to be with me for one reason or another. I figured I'd go off to college and really let loose. Megan and I were gonna get an apartment with this other girl we know, party every night."

Jonathan found the feeling of isolation melting into one of abandonment. Was there really a world out there where things like this were going on?

"Then you had to show up."

She fell quiet then, the room filled with the screaming silence.

"I think I'm still in love with you."

The words hit his chest and resonated.

"I know that's a really fucked up thing to say. I think it's because of Megan. You were there for me, not just tits and a pretty face, and not my hot friends, but me, and when you left a part of me woke up." Again the mattress creaked and she came over the side of the bed, snuggling in beside him and laying her head on his chest. He could feel the soft movement of her breathing.

"Do you still remember me?" She asked in a whisper.

"Yes."

"Do you still love me?"

"Yes."

Then she was kissing him. Soft kisses, the kind they'd shared one rainy evening with his old friend Mr. Hazelwood looking on. Kisses from a time when innocence was still king, where the world was still new, and she was Emily to him again. In those moments, when he allowed himself to forget all she'd said, all the things that now made her, her, it was okay. They stopped and looked at each other, two people crossing paths yet another time in their lives.

Emily took his hand. Before he could grip it she put it beneath her shirt. For a moment he felt himself waking. Then she slid the hand down, stopping just below her navel. He waited for something. When nothing transpired he looked up.

Emily stared back, eyes searching. Jonathan saw desperation and he also thought sadness. As his realization dawned, she gave a small smile and he knew. Even before the words came out he knew.

"I'm pregnant."

His first thought was, "whose?" After the stories she'd told him there was no idea. Emily knew though, knew more than she'd known anything else in her life. It was his. When she told him he only stared, letting the shock absorb into what it would. What took its place was a mixture of happiness and contentment, so unexpected he felt himself trying to cry.

Now that he looked close he could see the small shape of her stomach pulling out from its normal sphere. He was about to speak when she cut him off.

"I'm not going to keep it."

The contentment was slapped from him. "What?"

"I can't have a baby, I'm barely eighteen."

"You're not serious?"

"I still have college. Kids come later, once I'm settled down. This train's just getting started." She tried to force a smile and realized present company didn't think her witticisms very funny.

"You can't just kill it."

"I can't have it. Who's gonna help me take care of it?"

"I will."

"We hardly know each other anymore."

"Is this why you came here, to get cozy and soften the blow?"

She sat up, pulling his hand away. "No, I meant everything I said. I still love you, Jonathan. I've never loved anybody else, but this is a baby. I'm not ready for a baby."

"Then give it to me."
"I can't."
"Why?"
"Because if it's here, I'll always be thinking about it."
"So this is your alternative?"
"You don't have a choice here, I'm doing this with or without you."

She took his hand. "Jonathan, listen to me. This is the best thing for everybody. You don't want to be stuck with me the rest of your life. I've done a lot of bad shit and you deserve better. I almost didn't come down here. I thought it would be easier if you never knew, but I couldn't do that to you. Please don't do this to me."

Jonathan didn't reply, he was hypnotized by the soft white of her stomach.

"Let's just go to sleep, we can talk about it in the morning."

He started to protest but he was suddenly very tired. After the final realization, all the energy had drained from him. All he wanted was to be away. Away from the chaos which was this girl, away from the chaos that was his life.

Emily lay down beside him and wrapped her arms around his chest. "I'm sorry."

Jonathan didn't reply, his mind was coming apart strand by tiny strand. Where there was once hope and wonder there was now concrete. Dead stone which did not give for any reason. It was in that place he found sleep and it was there he remained while at three in

# KINGDOM

the morning, Emily slipped out of his bedroom and out of Morning Ridge.

When he woke, he thought the whole thing was a dream. There was no angel of a girl lying on his chest. No aroma of her hair. What he found instead was a note, one single piece of paper with four sentences on it.

"Jonathan, I'm sorry. Don't worry about me or anything else. I'll take care of it. Stay happy and try to remember me the way I was. Emily."

When he found himself at the creek, he knew why he'd come. It was the final straw, the final act of defiance from a world which would not let him be happy. With each thought he tore the note, piece by piece, until it was nothing more than summer snowflakes in his palm. This time he didn't have to throw it in, a gusty breeze picked them up and danced them along their path to the water. Instead of climbing in and floating away he stepped to the middle and looked into the cloudless blue, thoughts of Arielle, thoughts of Bailey. A girl with blonde hair and a baby he'd never see. No more.

As the paper drifted away, Jonathan began to scream. It wasn't one of fear or terror, but one of solidified anger. The sound carried into the august greenery painting the sky with birds and an echo which seemed to resonate long after he was gone.

Down the street he went, past houses he no longer saw. The cemetery was deserted as it always was, except for one man who sat on the park bench reading an old paperback novel and eating a sandwich. In his mind's eye he saw the dead rising over that specter's back as they'd done in his drawing, vying for the sky and paying little attention to the man before them, lost.

Arielle's grave was at the back of the church, along the bedding of flowers in the newest section of the cemetery. Their mother had put a bouquet of flowers in the vase and a small white angel by her name. Jonathan knelt, clearing off the excess grass that grew across the edges. She had been his only real friend, the first in a long lineage of things which should have been but would never be again. There was no reason she should be out here, no sense of anything.

"It's me sis. Just came by to say I love you."

And he stayed with her for awhile, telling her about Mr. Hazelwood, the jars. Everything that had happened spilled out in whispers and tears. The sheer urgency of the need to see her, the unquenchable desire to laugh with her again, to have her tell him that it would all be alright, that it was all just a bad dream, ate his soul. Her eyes, so clear and beautiful, would never shine on her baby brother again, would never see another picture or a perfect summer day, and Jonathan didn't want to be anymore. Didn't want to know what it was to breathe and keep going. He wanted to be away from himself, away from it all.

With no clear thought save the one which went, "I have to make this stop," Jonathan walked back across the headstone littered lot. Brady Coleman looked up from his paperback, gave Jonathan a short glance, and went back to his reading. "He's the one that does the digging." Jonathan thought. "The one who covers us with earth, and in the end he supposed it would be enough.

He crossed the empty street and headed back towards the only home he'd ever known. Had he ever really mattered? Had anything? Life stretched out before him in a long unknowing lineage which he could not bear to go through. So many days, so many endless hours of regret and longing that wouldn't be filled with living but with alternate forms of existence that were only formalities to those involved. Even if he did find a reason to move on, such was not his choice. Time it seemed killed everything, everything except the love of what you'd lost. .

# Chapter Twenty

Emily rode out of town in the car her mother had bought her, a fully loaded Benz with brown leather seats and a radio that was the envy of all the boys. With Morning Ridge at her back, she felt better. There was no way she could stay there; no way could she have this baby.

When she missed her period two weeks after Jonathan had come, no pun intended, she chalked it up to coincidence. Why she hadn't made him use a condom, she'd never know. Maybe it was his eyes, maybe their history. Whatever the reason, it had been a stupid one. She'd taken a test and stared in wonder at the little pink plus. She'd almost gone out right then and done it, the clinic was open and she had the cash but a little voice wouldn't let her.

In the end, she couldn't do it without talking to him first. Only they hadn't really talked about it. She'd said she was going to do it and he'd protested. It was too late to worry about it now. Once it was taken care of, she could rejoin the world. Jonathan would never fully leave her but she knew he was better off without her. She'd picked up more than one bad habit and quite a few more skeletons. The one's she'd showed him were just the tip of that iceberg.

There was a time when she felt bad about the things she did, a time when her conscience still shouted loud enough for her to hear. But that had been long ago. With each act of defiance, whether towards her parents or towards herself, the nagging sensation faded. Now she could pretty much do what she wanted without it yelling at her and yet, it was yelling at her now.

Jonathan had a way of waking up her senses. Somewhere deep down a part of her was sleeping. She'd sung it a lullaby and sent it on its way. Yet every time he was around it stirred, rolled over like some damned beast, and it was dangerous to the current situation. She turned up the radio trying to drown out the thought. "That's the fucking trouble with your head." She thought to herself. "You can't turn the damn thing off."

At seven that evening she pulled into a parking lot outside the apartment she'd soon be living in and found Megan sitting on the balcony.

The girl looked down at her from her perch. "About time you got here."

Emily pulled her duffel out of the oversized trunk. "I'm two hours early."

"Yeah, about time you got here."

The apartment was unfurnished, except for a blanket Megan had brought to sleep on. The rest of the things would arrive on Saturday fully equipped with moving men.

"So?" Megan was standing in the kitchen trying to open a can of peaches.

"So what?"

"So what did he say?"

"Not much."

The sound of metal popped as the can peeled back. "Am I gonna have to beat it out of you."

Emily sat down on the floor and leaned against the sliding door. "He wants me to keep it."

"Told ya."

"Shut up."

"Well I did." She poured the peaches into a small bowl, one of two in the place, and came into the small den. "That kid's crazy about you."

"I know, but I can't have a baby."

"I know you can't." Megan took a bite of peaches.

"Besides, you don't know him anymore. That thing at your parents was a major fuck up. You should have wrapped him up better."

"I know, but it was just Jonathan, you know. That sweet little boy I remembered."

"You're crazy."

"Yeah, I know."

"Well, I guess the quicker you get it over with, the better off you'll be. You got an appointment tomorrow right?"

"Eight-thirty."

"Well, get it done and then get back here. I'll have Mr. move-it-man put your bed up first. That way you can rest."

Emily hugged her. Megan held the fork up and Emily ate the peach off the end. "Those are good."

"Got some more in there if you want."

"I think I'm just gonna go lay down."

"Wanna borrow my blanket?"

"No, I got one in my bag."

"I'll be in after I finish these." Megan held up the half empty bowl. The peach sections shifted in the syrupy juice.

Emily went down the hallway. The corridor was dark but the room was lit by a street lamp from the parking lot. This was going to be her place for the next six months. She saw it filled to capacity with kids and fun, music blaring, beer flowing, kisses lashing, bedrooms full. It would be a non-stop party. She saw it all with perfect clarity. Saw the inhabitants stoned out of their minds with freedom and uninhibited playtime, saw puking and bongs and lunatic laughter but she saw something else as well, a boy with sad eyes standing alone in the dark. A boy with dark hair pushed back from his forehead looking at her with eyes too old for their years.

That night she dreamed she was walking down

Baker Street with him. It was dusk and the soft shadows of evening stretched out before them in elongated patterns. The boy was smiling, talking about everything and nothing at the same time. It felt good to be with him, it felt safe.

They wound to an old creek bed once flowing so hard she'd almost been swept away. She could remember how he'd pulled her back, how they'd stayed out all night, and how her parent's hadn't even noticed she was gone.

They crossed to the other side and up the embankment. She turned to ask where they were going but the boy was gone. Looking up she saw an older version, the one she'd just seen hours before walking a few feet in front of her, head down, hands in his pockets.

It was their place he was leading her too; only he wasn't leading her. She was following him, time turning in on itself. Though it was dark, she saw him ascend a small series of stairs. The scene began to swim as she saw the front of the door he was trying to open. A makeshift sign hung above it. There was a word written on it but she couldn't make it out. The door swung open and she saw a large metal container sitting just inside the entrance. It had words on it too, but she didn't need to read them to know what it said, "Gasoline".

The uncovered window faced east and as morning came it painted the girls with light. Megan rolled over, pulling her blanket over her head. Emily hadn't gone to sleep in the most thought out position. Her exposed face caught the light, bringing her back from the dream she wanted so badly to finish. She sat up, the intensity of it still lining her brain. It was bad that she'd been pulled from its grip but at the same time it was good. She had an appointment to keep. She got up, stepped over her sleeping companion and went to the kitchen.

The other can of peaches was still there so she indulged. As she ate, she watched the remainder of the sunrise. There was something growing inside her, busy eating the peaches she'd just consumed. A little piece of her and Jonathan which would, in an hour, be stilled. She popped the final peach in her mouth and bit down, savoring the sweet texture as she swallowed.

The clinic wasn't far from their apartment. The lot was too full and the inside too bright. She went up to the counter and a girl, not much older than her, handed her a clipboard.

"Fill out the front and back of this. When you get finished, bring it and your insurance card up with you. I'll need to make a copy."

Emily picked a seat by the window, filling out the information on her current health. At the end was consent for counseling box which she had to check. She signed her name and took it up to the girl. Formalities aside, she sat back down.

Ten minutes before her appointment an odd sensation began to creep over her. She wasn't sure where it was coming from but knew it had been started by the eyes of a girl who'd come out the back and left. There was a look on her face that haunted Emily, a look of decisions made too late. Was she really going to kill their baby? The dream occurred to her again, the dream with the beautiful boy who brought calm. There was something else he filled her with, a deep ache in her chest. What the hell was wrong with her? She was stronger than this. Then she realized something she hadn't expected. She really was stronger than this.

"Yes, can I help you?" The check-in girl asked.

"Would it be alright if I rescheduled?"

"Is something the matter?"

"No, it's just, well I just moved here and all my stuff is coming today. They were supposed to be there yesterday but their schedule got messed up. I don't want to be sick around strange men."

The girl smiled. "When would be a better time for you?"

Emily found she was no longer fully in control. "I'll have to call you back."

Then she was out the door. The flood of emotions that greeted her made her sway and she had to reach out against the building to keep from falling. When she reached her car, she fell inside and began to cry. It was the deepest and hardest purging of emotion she'd ever done. Cradling her stomach she spoke two words over and over again, the hard sky an ocean of blue above her.

"I'm sorry, I'm sorry, I'm sorry."

# Chapter Twenty-One

Jonathan had been going to their place for three months now, long enough to get over the initial shock of Emily. It was nearing mid-September and the grass was beginning to die. There was a large circle around the generator where he'd spilled gas many times and everything there was dead. He could smell the stink of it, so willing to be set ablaze, and he smiled to himself. The days were becoming shorter and he could taste fall in the air. It wouldn't be long before there was a much larger circle of death.

He came around the front, can in tow and ascended the rickety stairs. The door was locked, with three dead bolts now instead of one, and he put the gas can on the small porch and extracted his keys. It took a few minutes but he'd gotten quite proficient with this part of his work. The final lock was turned and he stepped inside.

With the help of the dying sun, there was plenty of light to see by. He walked to the single bulb he used for illumination and pulled the chord. In its light, he could see a variety of paint cans sitting on the floor. He bent to pick one up and set it on the small table at the edge of the room. Using a screwdriver, he began prying off the lid.

The floor was his focus today. The soft brown of the wood was being covered with a bright white sheen. He was using flat paint, not latex, but the smell was still strong in the enclosed room. The thought of doing the floor was silly at first, but he'd decided he wanted everything to match. It would be better that way when he moved to the final step.

The walls had been another matter. The first problem he ran into was that they were too exposed to the outside. There were holes and cracks running along almost every beam. Not only was it detrimental to what he was doing but it let in the elements. After careful consideration he approached Mr. Baker and asked permission to perform some maintenance. The man told him he didn't see any reason to fix up a place he intended to tear down once his lawyers got done with those tree hugging "son's a bitches" but if Jonathan wanted to do it, "knock yourself out," he'd said.

# KINGDOM

So he'd borrowed his father's truck and bought some drywall, returning through the back entrance to the field. It felt sacrilegious driving to their place, he always believed there was no other way except through the creek, but really, what did it matter, they'd be tearing the place down soon.

He'd never done drywall before. The hardest part was moving the pieces in without having any help. He decided cutting them in two was his best bet. He'd get one in, then set the piece he'd cut off back into its original position and start nailing again. Eventually, he was able to move much more efficiently.

The next step had been the mudding. He'd bought a mask and an electric sander and emerged every night like a ghost, moving to the creek to wash himself off before going home. The secrecy and lack of sleep had taken its toll, his paranoia had increased and he quit interacting with anyone unless it was absolutely necessary.

Now, as he began painting the floor he looked on those days with weary determination. As the night drew on he stopped dipping the brush and simply poured pools of paint. By three that morning he'd painted himself to the door. The fumes had lifted his head and he wasn't quite in the world. The sensation faded with each breath as he came out on the porch. There had been a light sheen of mist on the walls which made him feel like dancing. So close now, four more weeks at most, a single month. The thought made him giddy.

He sat on the steps and leaned back. In the sky an

odd mixture of starlight, moonlight, and the hint of sunrise looked down on him. Thoughts of Emily came and he fought to push them away. The last week he'd tried contacting her to no avail. He managed to get her number at college but when he called, her friends would tell him she was out, in the bed, in the shower, or on a pilgrimage. Once he thought about going down and physically not allowing her to do it, but he wasn't too sure that would matter now. The last time he'd talked to Megan she had said, "Don't worry about it she's already taken care of it. Just move on."

After she'd hung up on him, Jonathan ceased calling. What was the point anyway? Their child was dead, just another addition to the travesties of the world. The world that had shown him sunlight on the coldest winter mornings, only to take it away before the warmth had time to settle. Each time he closed in on something, the one thing that would make everything better, another piece of his heart was broken. So really, what did it matter? He had his walls, he had his secrets, and when the time came, he had his gasoline.

By the end of the week, the floor and ceiling gleamed. Jonathan found himself at home less and less. He'd begun sleeping in their place. With no outside light, he'd sometimes sleep through the day. Darkness became his solitude. When his mother asked about his odd behavior he'd said, "It's a surprise," and oh yes, what a surprise it was. By the following week most of what he'd wanted to accomplish was finished, stretching before him like a bastion of eternity. This was his, every inch of it, and before the end of October, he would come out no more.

When Emily arrived in Morning Ridge, not sure how to proceed, Jonathan was well into his final act. She'd decided not to contact him directly, fearing he would be angry with her. Instead she taken to following him, realizing how this action mirrored their first encounter before things like abortion and deception became part of their lives.

Every day she'd watch him go down Baker Street, head down, hair blowing and each night she'd wait in the shadows as he'd emerge. On the third day, she managed to get close enough to get a good look at him. Once upon a time, and not so long ago, that face had been full of life, a face where expressions grew straight and wonderful. The apparition before her now was a mere shell of that angel. Black lines under his eyes, hair and clothes unkempt, and he'd lost weight, she'd guess at least ten pounds. She wasn't sure what was going on, but there was something wrong with him, something very wrong.

By the fourth day she'd gotten his routine down. He would come out to their place at dusk, stay until the sun rose, then return to his parent's house where he would stay for a few hours alone before reemerging to walk the streets of town. This last event was one he'd only begun to indulge in. With the completion of his task so close at hand, he wanted to make a point to reflect. Where there was once cold bitter uncertainty and limitless change, he now saw only ghosts of himself. One woman who passed remarked to her husband about the scary young man, for the smile he wore was void of happiness, manifested by the cold solidity that this place no longer held any power over him. All its changes and all its pain would soon be memory.

And so it was on a Friday, he came out and Emily decided to go in. It was risky but she was worried about him. Either he'd gotten himself a habit, or he was sick. Whichever was true she had to know so she parked her car and waited for him to emerge. Around four in the morning he came out of the woods and began heading away from her. When he was far enough down the street, she opened her car door.

She had no trouble remembering the way. The old place still stood where it always had, a monument to the vastness around it. She knew it was where he'd been coming. She marveled at how new it looked. The stairs were dark but enough light shone to find the door knob. It would unlatch, but would not open, an assortment of locks saw to that. Why she ever believed it would be so easy, she didn't know. She turned to head back to the car. When she did the sound of rustling leaves and faint whistling resonated through the darkness. She ran behind the building and hid in a small outcropping of trees.

Jonathan passed close enough for her to smell the aroma of paint on him. At least she knew why he looked so bad, 'sniffing paint all night out in the field', she thought, "Who would have guessed."

He reached down and fired up the generator. It screamed and began chugging along. She waited until

# KINGDOM

he'd gone up the steps before slipping in on the east wall. Peering around the side she could see a small triangle of light and smell the pungent smell of paint. She edged closer and saw a red can just inside the door and recognized it for what it was.

She jerked back as Jonathan came on the porch. He locked the door and headed back down the stairs.

"He's lost his mind", she thought, then another thought. "Not spray paint." She knew a thing or two about huffing but had never heard of doing it with house paint. It was probably possible, but not very sensible. When he came back she would confront him. Why she hadn't already was her own stupid fear. Now his life was on the line and that affected her plans, added more complication to the complication she'd brought. She waited a few more minutes before returning to her car.

When he came back some four hours later, she'd fallen asleep. He passed unknowing as he always did, headed back into the woods with an empty jar and three containers of paint thinner.

The next morning the car felt like an oven. When she woke bathed in sweat, an old couple stood looking at her from the sidewalk. Emily smiled at them and started the car.

There was no way to tell if Jonathan was still across the street and it didn't matter. She couldn't keep watching him and wondering what to do, she wasn't fifteen anymore. She took the familiar path to his parent's house and pulled in the drive. This was the real deal, no turning back now.

She rapped against the wooden frame and waited. Nothing. No good. She reached out and pressed the doorbell. There was a low bing bong, and when no one answered she pushed it again. This time the door opened before she could take her finger off the button.

It was Jonathan's father, glasses low on his nose, paper under his arm, the old familiar constant. There was a look of confusion then a smile. "Well I didn't expect to see you out here this morning."

"I'm looking for Jonathan, is he around?"

"Don't see much of him these days. He's got an apartment he rents in town. I'm not really sure where."

"Did he tell you about us?"

"Not much, just that you had to get back to school and he didn't think you'd be coming around anymore. He'll be really happy to see you."

Emily smiled. "Yeah, I'd really like to see him too."

"Oh, look at me, where's my manners? Come inside, I was just having some coffee."

They went into the kitchen where there were two places set. "I was just about to go wake up his mom."

Emily sat down in Jonathan's seat. "Is he okay?"

His father stopped. Waking the wife wasn't such a good idea anymore, this was a sore subject. "There's something going on with him, yes."

"Is he sick?"

"Not with a cold or anything like that." He paused

for a moment trying to find the best way to convey it. "Jonathan's been through a lot and I think it's finally catching up with him."

"I'm sorry."

"No need, nothing anyone could do. Life is how it is."

"Well I think I might have had a little to do with it."

He smiled knowingly. "You can't beat yourself up. People have to live their own lives." He took a drink of coffee. "For what it's worth though, I think you made the right decision."

Emily realized he was looking at her stomach, it had a noticeable bulge. When their eyes met she could only smile. "I hope so."

From upstairs the sound of footsteps resonated. Emily looked questioningly at the man.

"Not him."

A moment later Jonathan's mother appeared, "I didn't know we had company."

"Yeah, she stopped by for breakfast."

Jonathan's mother looked toward Emily. "Have you seen him?"

"No."

"He looks a little different. Things on his mind I think."

Emily nodded.

"My goodness, how far along are you?"

"About three months."

"Do you know what it is?"

"No."

She looked at her husband, seemed to smile, then sat down. "Maybe you can talk some sense into him. He won't talk to us."

"Is he coming home today?"

"We're not sure. I think he watches the house."

"Why would he watch the house?" Emily asked.

"So he knows when we're home."

"He comes in and eats when we're gone." His mother said. "Sometimes he takes a nap on the couch, I know because he never cleans his mess."

"We keep trying to get him to see a doctor."

"Well something has to change with him. I've never seen him like this."

The three of them sat in silence, his parent's reflecting on their son and Emily trying to figure out how much of it was her fault.

"Do you mind if I stay here and wait on him?"

"That's fine. Julia and I were going to see a movie a little later on, so you'll have the place to yourself."

They ate breakfast, talking the talk of general life and situations without any sign of Jonathan. When eleven-thirty rolled around Emily moved her car to the back of the house and watched as Jonathan's parent's headed down the street. They'd be gone for three hours, plenty of time for her to talk to him alone, plenty of time to try and explain.

# Chapter Twenty-Two

Jonathan did watch the house though not as frequently as his parents thought. When he came up the sidewalk he was surprised to see just the truck parked in the drive. Gone somewhere, it didn't matter where, he wouldn't be here long. Jogging across the front lawn he ascended the steps and brought out his house key. He slipped through the door and into the kitchen.

There were a couple pieces of cold bacon on the stove and he stuck both in his mouth before squatting to rummage under the sink. He didn't see Emily standing in the shadows.

There were stains on the back of his neck, either blood or mud, and his hair didn't look combed or washed in a long time. With each slam of the drawers she flinched. Maybe it was a bad idea after all. The apparition before her was mad, had to be mad, then he turned towards her and she got a glimpse of his eyes. Not mad, sad, utterly disposed of happiness.

How he hadn't seen her she didn't know. He'd looked right at her and returned to his rummaging.

"Jonathan?"

The mad pulling and slamming stopped. The boy's head cocked like a dog who's hearing its master's voice. When he turned she stepped out of the dark and for a moment, Jonathan thought she was just another dream.

"Jonathan, it's me."

He found himself staring into a face he knew he would never see again. Dead to him, that's what she was. Now here she stood and what did it all mean? A part of him wanted to ask, needed to ask, but an even stronger part of him wanted to be out of there.

"Say something," the voice so full of life and totally untouched by misery. She came forward and he backed away.

"What's wrong?"

"Everything." His words were hoarse.

"What are you doing out there?"

Jonathan felt an odd sense of exposure, a sense he'd been uncovered. "What do you know about it?"

"I've been watching you."

He spoke through clenched teeth. "Why?"

"Because I'm worried about you and..."

Before she could finish he was across the floor. The screen door flapped closed as he ran across the yard. He fell once, righted himself, and disappeared down the sidewalk.

Anger flew through him. Why that one? Why now? All his hard work and to have been watched by her! He didn't think she knew what he was planning but the fact that she had even been there, stealing what was his. It belonged to him. It was the only thing he had left. It was not meant for her eyes.

He crossed from pavement to dirt and into the creek. The current was fast and the force knocked him down. Water sprayed in lunatic arcs as his knees came down on rock and he felt a scream escape his lips. He came up on the other side, still running. Ascending the steps there was a horrible moment when he thought he'd left his keys, but he checked his back pocket and found them easy enough. Then he was through the door, throwing all the locks behind him.

The best of his work was on a table sitting cockeyed in the center of the room. On top were his charcoals, the ones Arielle had given him. Beside everything were her notebooks. He'd opened one to his favorite passage, the one that helped lead to his revelation, the one that gave him the courage to go on.

"About that time," he said though no one was there to hear. "I hope you're ready."

The gas can was sitting on the floor next to his feet and he nudged it. It returned his affection with a deep slosh. "I know I am."

There was a long piece of white board propped up against the wall. Jonathan sat down next to it and painted a single word across it. "Well old fella, you're my epitaph, and a suitable one at that." He set the wood aside and went back to the door. Everything was ready now. A break was well deserved. He peeked through the small hole he'd inserted in the door and looked around. No sign of Emily.

As night fell, and he began to get hungry, there was still no sign of her. Jonathan checked his watch and decided he had a little time to eat. There were some peanut butter crackers in a bag by the table and he brought them out. He sat on the floor and opened a can of warm root beer. The combination wasn't the most appealing thing, but he wasn't eating for the pleasure of it, he just wanted his strength back. The mixture went down slow and he could feel his stomach beginning to growl, "hungrier than I thought I suppose."

When the eating was done he checked the peephole again and saw no sign of anyone. He'd probably scared the hell out of her looking and acting the way he did, not that he cared much. She'd killed their baby and had come to either find absolution in his forgiveness or to ask for some other favor that he would be unable to provide. Whatever the reason it was time for her to feel helpless. It was his time to finish the one thing that he had the power to finish. He unlocked the door and stepped out onto the porch. She wasn't hiding in the wings waiting to spring forth on him. The opening found nothing but the quiet of another night. He walked slow back into the room, knowing it would be the last time he did it, and picked up the piece of wood.

He walked back to the porch, picked up a rock from the edge of the stairs and brought a nail from his pocket. Trying to keep it level he drove it through the center of the wood. It stuck to the large door easy enough. When he let go, it turned slightly to the right. Jonathan decided he liked it better that way. "More interesting." Then he was inside, and in the midst of moving on.

If he'd been more of a lookout, he would have seen Emily standing on the far side of field. It wasn't a place where she could see him well, but it was a place she could see him.

Inside, Jonathan locked the door and was moving towards the center. The table still stood with all his things intact. He fumbled through the array of brushes, some in paint thinner, some lying dry, and picked out one he'd cut to specification. The final movement must be done with precision and there were no brushes save this one that he'd trust.

The room, much different than it had been when he rented it, had become his salvation. It had been a labor of love that started with a primer coat and closed with the floor. It took three coats before no wood grain poked through. He'd layered on a fourth for good measure then systematically continued the process around the room. The ceiling was the hardest to complete due to its irregular shape and age. There were holes that needed to be fixed and it slowed work by a few days. It took three weeks in total to cover the entire interior of the studio with primer. It took awhile for it to dry, and the smell was horrible, but he'd let it air out over a few sleepless nights and when it was done he had what he wanted, a perfect blank canvas.

He'd gathered up his sketches and positioned them along the floor, trying to determine the best starting place. There was a flow that needed to be identified and if he didn't get it right he would have to start the process over again. The first thing he decided on was a field. It stretched along the front and side walls with perfect symmetry. The small structure that stood in the center of it had begun to rot away. It was the way he'd seen it years before, when the small hovel had been a brown scar against the beautiful back lit afternoon. It was the beginning of summer, and the air tasted clean. Discovery was the cornerstone of his early life and this had been his Egypt, this bright place of green and blue, the place where he learned to draw, the place she loved to write, captured now, thrown from his mind onto the wall of this place with photographic perfection.

Connected to this image with no visible division was a house. It towered high above the lot it sat on with a man on its steps, a cigar between his lips. Bailey Hazelwood stared down Baker Street, a hand to his forehead to shield the sun. There was no sickness in him, his shoulders tanned and muscular against the white fabric of his shirt. Bailey's had been the last wall to dry.

# KINGDOM

The first one stood behind him, but it would be the last one finished. All the images along that wall met into a single mural. There was no way to tell where one scene ended and another began. The central point of all these was another house. It was the house he'd grown up in, the place where sounds of laughter always resonated until the world had gone. It was the birthplace of his dreams, the interior makings of a young boy who longed to be grown and once that place was reached, longed to return to its security.

In the yard a figure stood. Her face was as tan as Mr. Hazelwood. She shone with brilliance against the deep green of the yard. The smile he'd drawn was one he'd remembered from countless hours alone with her, countless days where the illusion of childhood was still so fresh you could taste it. In this rendering there was no touch of cancer, no touch of gauntness in the face, no thinning hair. This was his sister before the evil descended, before the world's hurtful spite drew in on her innocence.

Arielle stared out at her brother, arms beckoning him to come. Beckoning him forward into a world he'd remember, a world where nothing was wrong with anything, a time when you stayed up late to watch movies and slept all day in warm sheets which were always soft, a place where you could still laugh without thinking about what other people thought, a place driven by love and hope and all the things which made us human. The only place he longed to be.

Soon it would be over, all the hurt and cold reminders. All the burning to see this place again, to see her again, the way it was. The way he thought it always would be. It was his blind love for something safe. For something which never asked for anything in return, yet it had stolen something from him. It had taken him prisoner. These walls were his windows, the shaking brush in his hand the rock, because now he could see it. It stood out so clearly to his trained eye. The place he'd left without realizing he'd done it.

One more pass and it would be done. The candy bar had been the first. Then the old wooden cars, the soup cans, the rocks, none of which had posed any issues. There was no real trouble until he tried to bring Biscuit through and it was that thought that made him hesitate.

He'd been six when his mother came in from an errand with the kitten in her hands. Jonathan had loved him instantly. They'd had a few good years before Biscuit disappeared but not before establishing itself in the framework a young boys mind. Jonathan wasn't sure why he'd thought about the cat so many years later, or why he thought he could bring the cat through, but it seemed like a harmless exercise.

There were no pictures of Biscuit, no likeness of him anywhere except in his head, but Jonathan thought he could get close enough. All the detail he could muster he put out on the page and it seemed that when he made the final stroke he had done a good job.

At first nothing happened. Jonathan thought he'd drawn something wrong until the animal's eyes rolled towards him. They were yellow and cold, blinking independent of each other. There was a wavering quality to the picture, and the animal beneath it swam. Before he could take in what was happening the animal leapt from the picture. The coloring changed as it passed from image into reality and the limbs, neck and nails were all twisted in insane directions. The animal hit the ground and hissed, rolling and frothing about.

Jonathan sat transfixed at the abomination writhing on the floor before him. It began to puke as it hissed and dug its claws into the wooden floor. He couldn't tell if it was aware of what was going on but he could tell that it was in pain. There was an old broom handle he used for stirring primer next to him and he picked it up, going towards the animal meaning to stop the horrid screaming. As he brought the stick up the animal turned its head towards him.

Until the day he died he would not forget the expression of contempt and knowing on the animal's face. It was as though the eyes of God, or of the devil, had focused in on this purveyor of creation. It continued to smile as Jonathan bashed its head apart. Even after the carcass had been removed, the hole dug, and the body buried, Jonathan could still feel the eyes on him. He brought out his book of notes and began to write:

"Theory Seventeen: The Art of Perfection. All things drawn with these tools must be rendered in their exact form. The human evolution that allows memories to change into legend also warps the reality of the thing which they originally were. Experiment 9, Biscuit, family house cat from age 6. I had no image of Biscuit except that image in my head, my memory, to guide my course. Where I could remember a haze of the creature, a portion of its impact on me, I was unable to render it completely. However, the image was still brought to life leading me to believe that not only is it capable of opening windows into this world, but it can also create its own worlds, thus creating hybrid forms across multiple plains. This is what I believed has happened with Biscuit. The parts of the animal I remembered were only part of the animal I drew and while I believe most of him was reborn, the remainder was filled in without the capacity to function and therefore was transformed into a monster I had to destroy. Even now, with the image closed, the window into this monstrosity has been locked as though it wants me to complete it, or to remember it, I'm still unsure which. This brings a new level of caution to the work I am doing here and I must heed the words of Mr. Hazelwood all the more now. I must be extremely careful."

He remembered this now as he came forward, the final act at hand. There was no hesitation, no sense of defeat. He had done everything that he could to make sure this scene was complete. Endless nights of study and reflection, the sketching, the drawing, the erasing, the starting over, it all had led up to this. If it went wrong, he would burn the world down, himself included, but if it went right...

The bristles touched the unfinished portion of Arielle's dress and made a quick swipe upward. The blue denim began to melt, shading itself and building depth. Another pass and the white was gone, caught in a million hues of fading blue. A final stroke brought completion. For a moment he waited, caught by the blinding brilliance of what he'd done. Then the breath caught in his throat. All around him the movement of life began. Wind, which hadn't existed before began to blow through the lush green of the sycamores towering above the mural of his parent's house and in this wind, her hair began to blow.

Jonathan turned, taking in the movement blossoming all around him. The grass of the field began to lay over under the gentle caress of the breeze. Jonathan's hair began to waver as it came out the wall behind him, to journey through the limitless sky before him. Then singing, soft and whimsical floated in behind him. He wanted to find that sound but before he could the smell of cigars drifted into his nose. He turned to see Bailey propped back on his arms.

Beyond the interior room, the sky was velvet. Emily stood at the top of the stairs. She could hear him walking around inside, but couldn't see anything but the faint outline of white somewhere deep in the darkness and she remembered her dream and found herself unable to move.

Inside the darkness she feared was a day unlike anything Jonathan had ever seen. Its brilliance rained warmth down on him. The sound of singing was clearer now and he recognized the voice. Somewhere deep in his mind he felt a knot trying to unravel. It was the way dreams made you feel when you woke and realized what you'd seen wasn't real. It was calmness, safety. He had a sudden thought that if he turned around, the knot would explode.

Emily continued to stand, switching from one foot to the other. She'd decided she'd go up and knock. If he wouldn't answer, she'd just wait. He'd have to come out sometime. It was a good plan but one she was having trouble executing. It was in the midst of this thought that she heard singing, and it wasn't Jonathan, it was a girl.

With some effort, Jonathan turned himself towards the sound. She stood with her back to him, the dress she wore familiar, picking pansies. With each one added to the group, she'd brush her hair from her face and start singing again. He could hear cars now, running up and down the street out of view, the sounds of sprinklers. Arielle continued to move, an animation he could hardly comprehend. All his living mind would tell him was that she shouldn't be doing that. It had settled itself into seeing her as picture Arielle, the still girl in the photographs. The simple animation of the real thing, the way her hands moved, her soft features, things he'd forgotten without realizing he had, all came rushing back to him with horrible force. The knot in his head began to unwind itself and he found it easier to breath, again unaware that it had become difficult.

Change had a way of tricking you into not knowing it was really there. It trudged along, wiping out little details, staying just out of view. Then one day you looked around and didn't recognize the landscape anymore. Didn't recognize that you'd gotten older and the people you used to love weren't going to live forever. It was smoke and mirrors distracting your attention while the important things slipped away. But Jonathan had seen it, seen it lurking beneath the dark with its teeth bared. Now he had the teeth and he meant to kill it where it lay.

Stepping forward he felt the air warm. Whatever he'd opened was spilling into the room like a screen door left open with the air on. The outside didn't rush in all at once. Beads of sweat began to form on his forehead, and she began singing again. The sound was so familiar, so natural, and as he was about to call out to her when she turned.

Emily thought she understood everything now. Jonathan wasn't down there trying to kill himself, he was shacked up with some girl. After all that talk of love and babies, he'd turned into her. The fear she felt for him began to fade. It was being replaced by an odd mixture of anger and an unexpected bit of jealousy. She wasn't going to go up there and knock, no, she'd wait until they came out together. That way there would be no door slammed in her face. No, "who is it", from the other side.

Jonathan found he couldn't move. Even if he wanted to turn away from her, he couldn't. Arielle held the bouquet of flowers in her hand, the soft song she'd been singing resonating in his ears. At first there was only confusion as she looked at him and Jonathan realized why.

"I'm older now." He thought.

Arielle didn't speak.

They stood, eyes locked. Jonathan tried to find the right thing to say and she only stared. It was her expression that broke his silence.

"It's me, Jonathan."

"Jonathan?"

"Yes, your brother."

"Why are you so old?" There was no accusation, just questioning.

"It's been a long time since you left."

"Since I left?"

"That doesn't matter now, we can go anywhere. Mr. Hazelwood showed me the way."

"Don't be blaming your troubles on me boy," a voice called from across the room. Bailey held up one hand and waved.

"Where are mom and dad?" Arielle was scanning the landscape for them.

"I'll bring them later."

"Bring them from where?"

"From home, I'll explain everything once they get here." Jonathan went to turn but she put her arms around his neck and hugged him. "I can't believe how big you are."

Emily thought she had it all figured out when the singing started. When another voice, this one male and much older than Jonathan, called out, all bets were off. She couldn't make out what the voice had said but she needed to know what was going on. Whatever had been holding her in place loosened its grip and she headed towards the stairs.

Jonathan stepped off the grass onto the floor of

their place. All his things were placed neatly in the center of the table and it only took one trip to grab them. The gas can sat in the corner along with a large black pressure sprayer.

He spun the black tip and depressed the lever. The smell of oranges was immediate. He raked the hose back and forth across the walls to the front and either side of him.

He sat the sprayer on the grass behind him and picked up the gas can sloshing gas along the floor of the room. When he thought he'd covered enough he simply put the can on its side. It rolled to the center of the room, vomiting gas.

Emily cut through the dark and saw a white sign hanging askew against the backdrop of a wooden door. She could read it now, even in the shadows of this place.

Once, a long time ago, she'd been in love with a boy who loved to draw, a boy who used to find happiness in the simplest of things. Something had happened to him along the way, this was proof of that. Whatever doubts she had about what he was doing, that solitary word struck fear in her heart. When the smell of gasoline began to fill her nose she began to pound on the heavy wood.

"Open the door, Jonathan! Open this fucking thing now!"

# Chapter Twenty-Three

Jonathan was halfway through the wall when a voice bellowed through the closed door. It was Emily, clear as day and mad as hell. Good. It would be a change for her, the wrong side of the situation. No doubt she thought he meant to burn himself to death. It was the conclusion he hoped all who visited the aftermath would come too. "Go away, Emily, nothing to see here!"

The matches were poised in his hands. Arielle knelt with her back to him, continuing to pick her flowers. The smell of summer flooded the rancid smell of gas.

"Open the door Jonathan, we need to talk!"

"No, I don't think we do. Things between us are done."

"You don't understand, just open the door and you'll see."

"I've seen enough, thanks."

He pulled the first match across the flint. It sparked but didn't light.

"Please!" She was crying now, the uncontrollable sobs of one who realizes it's too late to stop something terrible.

Jonathan ignored her. It was the damn wind that kept blowing the matches out. He turned towards the back wall being careful not to step into the pool of waiting liquid.

Emily began to slide down the door. In a second she would be on her hands and knees. It was her fault after all wasn't it? She was the one who left in the dead of night without a word except, "I'm killing our baby."

"Please." The word came out as a whisper.

From above her, the sound of locks being thrown flooded her ears. She waited for the door to open but instead heard someone walking away from it. She pushed the door as the match in Jonathan's finger lit. The flame sputtered, imprinting itself on his eyes as it dropped with seamless grace, landing in a pool of gas. Fire shot up, coating the room in orange light.

As the door slid open, the light from the fire danced along the doorway illuminating the shadowed sign. In its orange glow Emily once again read the word painted there feeling chills run down her spine, "Kingdom."

The walls were wavering but she could still make out what they were. It was as if Jonathan had stolen pieces of the world and made a room out of it. She wasn't sure if the illusion was caused by the intense heat but she had an idea it was only part of it.

Jonathan had no idea how she'd gotten the door open. Behind licking flames he could see the determined face of a girl he once loved. He saw what she meant to do and he had to stop her.

"Don't!" He yelled, but she didn't listen.

She ran towards him, feeling the touch of a small wall of flames along her legs. In a few more minutes the walls themselves would catch and the whole place would be a prison of fire. She meant to grab him and pull him out, to hell with what he wanted. She wasn't going to let him kill himself. When she got close enough to see him without the illusion of flame, she stopped. Jonathan wasn't standing on her side of the wall. He'd gone into it somehow.

Jonathan saw her comprehension and his own flooded in. How he'd missed it before he had no idea. The soft section beneath her breasts had a visible rounding to it. She hadn't killed it.

Emily followed his eyes and was relieved to see joy in them. Then she was being pulled forward, the heat was replaced by gentle breezes, and the hard floor she'd been standing on had somehow turned to grass.

Jonathan sat looking at her in his parent's front

yard. She had no idea how that was possible but it was. When she turned around she could see the fire still blazing. Part of it was licking up onto the place where the concrete ended and the grass began.

"Move back." A voice said from behind her. She did and smelled oranges. A wide spray of juice was hitting an invisible section of the world. It stuck to it, unlike the fire, and began to run down. As it did, the scene behind it froze as though it were a photograph. The more the juice ran, the more the heat subsided. As the sprayer in Jonathan's hand began to sputter, the place in front of her was once again a wall. Except that wasn't quite right either. It was like a large picture sitting in the middle of the yard. She could see sky over it and grass to either side of it but the rectangle which made up fire and the room beyond stood solid.

She detected movement behind him and was shocked to see a young girl picking flowers. "Who's that?" But she found she could answer that. Who else would it be? Then his hand was on her stomach, his eyes wide with excitement.

"You didn't do it?"

She smiled at him, "No."

And he kissed her. It was so unexpected she almost fell backwards.

"This is perfect, I was gonna try to bring you in, but this is better, this is real."

"And what is this place?"

"My memories. The place I've been trying to get back to my whole life."

"But how?"

"That would be my fault." A voice from behind them said. Bailey came around the corner of the fire painting, hands in his pockets. "See, I showed him how to make his pictures live. Nice place he made for us don't you think?"

Jonathan was looking at the man with gleaming eyes. "You let her in didn't you?"

"It was obvious to me she needed to tell you something. By the look of her, I'd say it was a good thing I did."

Jonathan turned back to Emily. "I want you to meet someone."

The girl picking flowers was still kneeling. When they got close enough, they saw why. A large black and yellow caterpillar was moving through the tufts of grass. It would run into her finger, pause, then head over it. The feel of its furry body made Arielle laugh. Jonathan touched her shoulder.

"Isn't he cute?" She said.

"There's someone I want you to meet."

Arielle waited for the insect to craw off her. She turned without caution or pause. Emily stood looking at the girl she'd seen only in photographs.

"Arielle this is Emily. She's a good friend of mine."

Emily took the young girl's hand, "She should be twenty-two," was the thought that came, but the girl in front of her was nowhere close. Jonathan's little sister was now younger than both of them.

The four of them sat in the grass, shaded by the

leaves of the massive poplars. The air was wet with flowers and freshly cut lawns. Jonathan began to talk, telling them first of the days after Arielle's passing, then moving to Mr. Hazelwood and the jars.

"I tried a few experiments before I realized the things in my head were just as alive as anything else in the world. The only difference was I couldn't give them solidity. The powder somehow opens a door between what you see, and how you perceive reality. I was able to create a window into them."

"So does it just stay like this?" Emily asked.

"I don't think so. I think that we've switched worlds. This is the one in my mind."

"Are you saying I'm just a projection of your mind? A moving picture?" Arielle asked.

"I don't think so. You're as real as I am, it's just you came out of another time if that makes sense."

"Exists in your head." Emily put in.

"Yeah."

Arielle pulled a stem from one of her flowers. "You're not finished yet are you?"

"Not yet. I didn't paint mom and dad in here because I wanted to bring them from the present. Then we can start over. You can grow up here, you can live your life here. Find someone to love and have kids. All the things that you deserved before they were stolen. I want us to be happy again, to be in this place without thinking about death. I want us to live as a family, grow old as a family, and when the time comes, move on as a family."

"So why did you bring me here?" Bailey asked.

"Because you spent the last years of your life alone. You deserve better than that."

"What about us?" Emily asked. "What about our baby?"

"It will be born into love, surrounded by family and two parents who adore it. Don't look at this as some other world that's unfamiliar. This is how the world should be. No one will be murdered here, there will be no disease. You will recognize everything from Morning Ridge. If you want to see other places we can cross back into the real world and go there. Once they're in our heads, we can make them here."

"So what do we do next?" Emily asked.

"We go get my parents."

The studio caught fire eight minutes after the match hit the floor. It blazed in the early morning with no one to see its fall. As the explosions of popping wood and shattering glass filled the air, the walls began to fall in on themselves, disappearing from the landscape as so many things, all things, would eventually do. By morning, there was nothing left of "their place" but a small pile of smoldering ash and a patches of dead burned earth.

# Chapter Twenty-Four

Jonathan's parents never woke when a small opening appeared at the foot of their bed. Sunlight poured in, drenching both from the knees down. Jonathan stood staring out into the dark. He stepped through, recognizing the smell of the room. There was no easy way to do it, no easy way to explain without showing them. The floor squeaked. His father grumbled something about being quiet then the room was lit.

"What the ..." his father began, and saw his son standing above him. The look of displaced anger was gone, replaced by one of confusion.

His mother was coming awake now, eyes searching for the source of her misery. "Jonathan, go back to bed."

"I can't, I have to show you something."

"Well what is it, can't you see it's..." She paused for a moment and looked at the clock. "Two in the morning."

"It'll just take a second."

His father stood up, looking for his slippers.

Behind them, the light from the opening slid to the left. Arielle was closing the door as requested.

"I need both of you."

His mother wanted to argue but she knew it was pointless. The three walked together, his parents in front, towards the closed door.

"It's right out in the hall."

Jonathan's father opened the door. Hard light flooded in and both were blinded. Jonathan pushed them. They went forward, arms flailing, cries of surprise escaping their mouths. Then Jonathan was through, the door closing behind him.

Both his mother and father were lying face down in grass as if they'd gone out of their bedroom directly into the back yard.

"What the hell's going on here, Jonathan?" His father asked.

His mother was trying to find her footing. A hand reached down to her. It was small, and she took it. She met her husbands eyes, meaning to follow his lead in retaliation, and saw them not filled with anger, but brimming with tears.

# KINGDOM

At first the sensations that overcame her puzzled her. There was no reason she should feel that way. Yet she'd followed his gaze, saw what he was looking at, and felt an onrush of emotion. It couldn't be real; she must still be asleep.

Through some miracle she couldn't begin to comprehend, her daughter stood before her. The soft face, her soft hair, things she had accepted she would never see again. Then Arielle was coming towards her, actually moving towards her, and she felt the blood rush out of her. Was it a dream? Then small arms were embracing her and the magnitude of the sensation sent her to the ground, a girl now herself, weeping.

Jonathan's father went to them, hugging both and crying. The three of them stayed that way for a long time. Emily took Jonathan's hand and put the other one on her stomach. If this was how it was to be him, she would stay here in this place.

Bailey stood at the edge of the yard, watching the mailman put letters in the box. As the truck drove away, he crossed the yard to retrieve them. Jonathan realized it had already started. Life was beginning to move forward again.

That night his mother would cook a huge dinner. Arielle would stand next to her, helping. Every so often her mother would hug her, if only to remind herself of that warmth of love. The food would be good, better than it had been in years. The parts of his mother which had died with Arielle had come back, revived by the sunshine in the little girl's eyes.

To Jonathan, it was the way life was supposed to

be. The familiar happiness he'd always associated with being alive. There was no anger in his heart, no hatred towards anything.

The night wound out. They told stories of the old days which had become the new days. Laughter rose as voices spoke and when twilight came, Jonathan went outside with Emily. He'd asked about her parents but she knew better. They were too much into the distractions of life.

As the rest of the world went to sleep, Jonathan finished a painting of a table and placed the jars inside. The thought came to him, at what point had the room been completed? If the paint did open a window into his memory then why could everyone else move through his thoughts, see the things he saw? He'd been so hell bent on creating the place he'd never really stopped to understand what it was. He knew how to control it, how to break into it, but this was the first time he himself had gone inside it. Everything seemed real, but what if there were other issues, things he hadn't planned for? There was a knock at the door.

"Yes?"

"Can I come in?" It was Emily.

"Sure."

Her hair was wet from the shower she'd taken. "You ready for bed?"

They lay together, the distant hum of the air conditioner filling the room. He began wondering again at what point the reality had become fantasy? What happened if he died? Would the whole thing fall? He rose and made his way to Arielle's room.

His sister was sitting on her bed.
"Arielle?"
She turned, eyes wet with tears.
"What's wrong?"
"I don't know."
He crossed to the bed and sat down with her.
"Can't you sleep?" He asked.
"No, I..."
"What's wrong?"
"Where did I come from?" He saw her confusion and felt his heart sink.
"What do you mean?"
"Mama was talking to me earlier, about when I was little, but I can't remember being little. I know who you are, and I know who they are, but I can't remember being little. The first memory I have of anything is crossing a field with you, going to write in my notebooks."
"Do you know how old you are?"
"Fifteen, but I don't know if that's right. What's the earliest thing you remember about me?"
He thought as far back as he could. "I remember you being small and taking care of me," but that wasn't the first thought that occurred to him. He had been eight years old the day they found their place for the first time, approaching it slow and reveling in the ancient mystery of it. Back then it had seemed so big, so full of life and discovery. It was the first thought that occurred to him, the only thought.
"You should try and sleep Arielle, it's been a long day."

"But that's just it Jonathan, has it been?"

"What do you mean?"

"There's nothing before today. I remember crossing the field, then I have all these memories of us and mama and school. I remember getting sick, and I remember dying. I can remember the pain and the tears and every one of you sitting around me holding my hand, and I can remember being scared, feeling alone and angry. Then I remember the dark. I was looking at everyone and black began filling my eyes and then I couldn't move but I couldn't wake and I felt myself dying. I can remember it so vividly Jonathan, the certainty of it, the fear. Then I was picking flowers in the back yard. I thought that I had gone to heaven, then you were there and I knew you hadn't died, or at least I didn't think you had." She stood and went to her door. "I'm going to call mama in here. I want you to stand where I can't see you, okay?"

"Okay, but why?"

"I just need you to explain something to me."

Jonathan did as instructed, standing in the corner of her room.

She called her mother, the sound so loud it hurt his ears. Within seconds she appeared. "What is it? Are you okay?"

"Yes, I'm fine. I just wanted to see you." She felt an odd mix of memories flood into her, ones moments before she could not recall. She saw herself as a baby, saw all the pieces of her that her mother had seen then she turned to Jonathan. He saw her turn towards him, saw how different she looked, and closed his eyes.

# KINGDOM

The memories that flooded through her came from his mother, the way that she'd known her daughter before he'd been born. All the teething and the play-pinning, the birthday parties, the scraped knees, but Jonathan did not exist then, was not in the world, and these new memories altered his perception of his sister. What he saw was not a beautiful vibrant girl, but a black faceless mass.

His mother noticed him and directed her attention towards his terrified gaze. "What's wrong with you?"

"Nothing" Arielle put in, "I just wanted to see you."

"Well okay." Her mother kissed her cheek. "You two don't stay up too late."

When he opened his eyes, his mother was gone and Arielle was back to the way he remembered. She came to him and knelt. "Did you see?"

"What was that?"

She smiled wearily at him. "Bailey told me you could open a window with those paints he gave you, and that a person or thing could cross in. The first time he crossed over he saw what I just showed you."

"He crossed over?"

"Yes, it's in the journal, the one in the picture."

"There was a journal? I never found a journal."

"It was at the bottom, under the table. He showed me."

Jonathan stood, meaning to go back to his room and get the picture but Arielle put her hand on his arm.

"He came up here while you and Emily were outside, brought it with him, said I needed to know what was really going on. He gave it to me to read. She brought it out and sat it on the bed beside him.

Jonathan picked it up, amazed at the worn cover.

"What does it say?"

"You need to read it for yourself."

There was fear in her eyes, a strange mixture of loss and confusion and he wondered how much of it was hers and how much was his own mind reflecting those expresssion through her. As if reading his thoughts she said, "Not all of it is you Jonathan, I am afraid."

He took the book from her and walked to window, sitting under the light of the summer moon. The pages were worn and the cover ancient, but the handwriting was familiar. Arielle lay back down in the bed, but never found sleep. Jonathan read through the night, crossing page after page in hungry swoops. As two in the morning came, Jonathan moved into uncharted territory. He recognized the passages on "Experiments" as new information and felt his mind widening against the true level of his limited understanding.

# Part III

Endgame

# Bailey's Journal
Experiments and Theories

# Chapter Twenty-Five

August 24th
The Theory of Perception

"What you must remember is what you create is determined upon all that you have seen. I've just returned from my first excursion into this new unknown. Terrifying as it may have been, I still found it useful. I have been taking notes thus far but will now document my findings in a series of journals. The basic premise is that what I know of this powder I can share with those who come after me, if I ever take it that far. My first expedition into the world of my creation was a stepping stone into my father's old house. It seemed a fitting approach for me to return to that place. On the other side of the painting I found the place to be exactly as I remember and that is why it is is so intriguing. There were things specific to my belief, and not only that, specific to my belief at the time. For example, there was a well there that I used to play around, enormous to my mind's eye as a child and yet when I came upon it here it was just as it had been. However, I am now a grown man now and the well still towered above me. It was my perception of the thing that caused it to be so. What I naturally mistook as tangible became part of me until the reality of the thing was changed. It appears based on perception. The paintings open a window into the self, whether it is a window into the current or into the past, it is still our perceptions that it opens.

I have decided that these jars, while powerful, do not open into a reality, they open into a belief, a need, a dream. I think the painting is only a reflection of our subconscious, and by being so is no more real when we are standing inside it than it is in our heads. It is merely a tangible reflection. Therefore, when we go into these paintings we go into ourselves. There is no return to the past, no time travel, merely a projector for the film in our heads.

We know that there is a motion of time and that all people are locked in this motion. Whether they change with a group or whether they forge their own path is the thing of life. I have seen many things that people I've come in contact with will never see, and even if they did, they would not be seeing them with me, nor would they see them in the same way that I see them. In that sense, one must realize that the powder is a lonely magic. Everything we see from the first moment we are born to the last moment before we die is inherently ours. I believe this is the reason we spend so much time talking and pressing our ideals on other people, we believe that none see what we see and in that unseeing we find ourselves alone. We run from that darkness every day of our lives. The powder gives the illusion that one is able to capture a utopia, a sort of Eden, making the wielder of this power a god in their own right. However, we must be aware that what we create is really a skewed view of reality, a reality to the level of (x).

The first level of this view is the true world, an actual physical tangible "law based" world that exists whether we exist or not. We put focus on the reflection of sounds by saying, "if a tree falls in the woods will anyone hear it?" This in itself is the quintessential reason man has found loss in the holding on of things. We believe that by our very existence nothing else can exist, as though when we were born the world began and when we die it will cease to move. That relationship with ourselves is the reason this magic is so attractive, it gives the ability to build a world that is only ours.

The second level is our perception of the world. This is the key to the magic, its ability to mimic ourselves. It is the layer, the paint, our memories on the canvas, the real world. What opens is creation of a new world, our world, and within that world everything is exact to our recollections. We have been building ourselves a land of our design to fit with the things that we believe, whether out of fear, or hope, or the need to control things, everything within us is a reflection of our souls perception on everything we touch, therefore the second level of the view is our level, the most important level. It is in the center of the real versus the third level where we reside, the balancing point, the center.

That level brings the problems with this magic into focus. What I perceive and what others perceive is apt to be as different as night and day. While some of the men in my battalion were able to handle the intensities or war, others were struck unmovable in situations. Where one man might find humor in a thing another might find confusion. When as a child I saw a monster in my closet, my father would see only a dark room. It was not the thing, the true thing, but the perceived threat of the same thing, so different in so many. This is the real trick of the magic. It allows us to capture and create a true world but a true world based on our perceptions. This introduced a fourth level which causes the balance to tilt, the (y) variable; the cause of unforeseen issues. Even if I could have drawn a picture of Camille and gone into it, what I would find is just my memory of her. I would in essence be stepping into myself, and though the place may trick my mind into believing that she is back, she would not be able to grow with me. She would be a thing of my creation, another piece of me, and would not be real.

## KINGDOM

The price we pay for these things is the need we have for ownership in a world that is in a constant state of decay. Nothing in the world truly belongs to us. We build ourselves a mountain based on everything that we've done, and we kill to hold on to it, not because we want the things to exist for their own good, but for ours. We are a selfish animal.

I have crossed back to the time of my mother who has long since been dust in the very earth I now stand upon. She could tell me of my life, of the things that I have done, but when questioned on the early times of her life, the things I most wanted to know about her, I found she could not answer me. There was nothing in this created mother that I could learn, nothing in her that wasn't in me.

The powder opens a door into the graveyard of our hearts. There is nothing new to be learned, nothing new to be experienced. Even if we move forward in that place we are not moving with the people and the places that we used to know. Those things are gone forever, at least within our abilities of recreation. One must not be fooled into believing that through a tangible, breathing entity we will find the thing that we know, because what we know is not them, but us.

From every person on the street to the people we interact with, we have given all their names. We have built our world around their existence without ever moving into their lives. Yet they perceive us much the same way. Surrounded by everyone, but we are alone. The movement of the world cannot be dictated by the needs of the singular. We all work in part to create a place based not only on perception, but reality. There is no balance through the powders use. There is only the reflection of. I say this not to detour the use of this magic, for it is a powerful tool in its own respects. However, the usage must be done with a clear understanding of its capacity and capabilities. One cannot use it as a means of replacement; it must be a means of remembering."

# Chapter Twenty-Six

December 5th:
The Degrading Reality Theory

"The passage of time is different inside. I have spent six months studying an old friend of mine who left when I was young. When the day came that he would have left I went to sleep believing that I would learn some great epiphany about whether these inhabitants can continue their lives within the created worlds. They can, and I think that was the most interesting part about the process. The boy that I had known continued along without much of a hitch, or so I thought at first. Careful observation proved that he was not the boy any longer, but a hybrid of the boy. At some point, probably after his true existence in my mind lapsed, there was a metamorphosis. I assumed some new powers. I could read his thoughts. Through concentration I also found that I could make him move or speak at my whim. From the point of my original knowing of him, he became dependant upon my perceptive creative ability. I had to give him life; I had to give him purpose, because he was in a very real sense, an extension of me.

Now some may find this appalling while others may find it intriguing. I found it made me sad. Did I want to exist in a place where there were no arguments, no bantering of ideas? In some respects, I could create an inhabitant who would do these things, but at the core I would be arguing with myself. As I have said, this magic is a selfish lonely magic and while the initial draw of it does help feelings of remorse and loneliness fade, these feelings are often reinforced, and with greater fervor, once the reality of the magic becomes apparent.

I cannot continue on my quest without further study. There is nothing but beautiful emptiness on the other side. The tragedy is that these places were only able to exist once, made up of all the people and places that came together in some beautiful when and where to form this wonderful and timeless moment in time. We have no capacity to recreate it in much the same way as we cannot bring love back just by wanting it to be so. We have to exist in the moment, in all its temporary beauty, and realize that we are there.

What made these places we long for so beautiful is the fact that we can't go back to them again. While we were there, we never noticed those moments of grace, those timeless conversations because we believed it would always be so. When it was taken from us we longed to return and we tried to rebuild and rework to no avail.

Once all that we've known is lost, it cannot be returned to us. We are destined to move, but we must be adamant in our quest not to fall victim to the very thing which consumes us. We cannot find true happiness by trying to find a place that is gone. The memory of that place is enough to sustain us and to further cement the fact that there can be places like that again, places with new walls and new people. For us to attempt to create these places is impossible. By their very design they are spontaneous and we may not even realize their existence until they are gone. This is the truth I have learned from the powder.

With that determination, I have decided to put these things away. There is nothing within them that I can find except loneliness and an unquenchable need for something I cannot create. Yet, even as I write and thoughts of destruction flow through me, I find that I am not able to pour out the powder and burn this journal. There are lessons here that others greater than me may be able to uncover, things that I have missed in my ignorance or a simple thought that has not come to me. I will however hide them away. I am closing this journal and moving on with my life.

## JEREMY RANDOLPH

There are too many things that lie forward than there are ghosts in the past. My moments will not be stifled by obsession of returning there."

# Chapter Twenty-Seven

Jonathan sat the book down. He could hear Arielle, what Bailey would have called an inhabitant, breathing soft. The wind began picking up, rattling the screen door in its berth. Was that wind a product of his mind? Was this entire place a product of his mind? Why hadn't he found the journal before he started? Why hadn't Bailey told him? He could remember the old man telling him to live his life, to go and not think about the jars. He understood now that Bailey had hoped he would find happiness through natural means and move past his sister, Emily. He hadn't thought Jonathan would be as stubborn as he was.

Bailey heard the knocking and rose. When he opened the front door, he saw Jonathan standing there.

"I suppose you want some answers?"

The two sat as they'd done so many times on the steps of Bailey's house. Morning Ridge stared back at them, the old trees still midway through their growth, but they were the way Jonathan had always loved them.

"Why didn't you tell me about the journal?"

"Do you really think that's the first question you should ask?"

"What's wrong with that one?"

"Well if I were you I'd want to know how I even remember the journal since I'm a product of your mind, and your mind knew nothing of it."

The thought hadn't occurred to him. "Okay, so what's the deal with that?"

"Well, you realize that the powder opens a door into your reality. It's the way you were able to bring out your car, the candy bar, etc."

"How do you know about that?"

"Because the layers here are inheritable, since I'm part of your memory, I am in a sense part of you. I have my own sense of self, because you brought me out of an existing point in time. I exist as a reflection here, but a reflection built on all I was. However, since you created this place, I am in essence a part of you and therefore I can see what you see."

"What else can you see?"

"That you are afraid."

Jonathan stared across the street. "What do I do?"

"That's not up to me."

"Why didn't you tell me it would be like this?"

"You wouldn't have cared. I'm not even sure you care now."

Jonathan knew he'd pulled the idea from his own heart so he didn't argue.

"If you look back on what I did, I tried to persuade you to learn of life your own way. I wanted you to go out and get beyond the loss. However, you always wanted to fix everything. Do you remember when I suggested you go see Emily?"

Jonathan did.

"I did that in the hope that you would go and see that she was still a person, and that you could still have a relationship with her. The person she was was gone, still is gone. As is the person you were. That's what I've always wanted you to understand. You've been so hell bent on making everything the way it was that you neglected to realize that you yourself prohibited that reality from ever occurring. You will never be as you were and therefore the place you want to return to cannot be made. It has gone, Jonathan."

"Why didn't you just give me the journal so I could know?"

"You can't tell anyone anything, Jonathan, especially someone as strong willed as you. You would have read what I wrote and believed that you could make a difference, that you could change it. You had to experience this first hand or you would cling to it the way you've clung to your past and would not be able to get past it. The lesson here is moving on son, you have to know that."

"But I have made this place and she is here."

"She is, but as you've read she cannot move past where she is now. She'll just be a reflection of you. It is the same with me. This version of me, when I reach the age of my death in your mind, everything that I know now, the journal, the days we spent, will fall away. All that will remain inside of me will be your mind, your control. You cannot create life Jonathan, you can only reflect it."

"So what can I do? I've brought mama, dad. I can't take her away from them again."

"I have no answers for you. You must explain to them what this place is. They can't be led to believe that they can stay here. You have already seen how your sister fades when you are together with her and someone else's memories."

"And if they refuse?"

"Then that is their choice."

Bailey sat listening to the rampant thoughts moving through Jonathan's head, the movements and the emotions tearing him apart. Then the boy looked at him.

"Are you angry with me?"

Bailey put his hand on his shoulder. "No. You had to come in order to see. It was the purpose of the lesson. Now you have to conclude the lesson, you have to set things right."

Jonathan waited until morning before approaching

his parents. He met with them in the kitchen, the smell of the morning and the heat of the day simmering around them. He started the story with the death of Arielle and continued on through the jars, the way he'd met Emily, all the loss he'd felt his whole life. Much of what he said came as news to his parents who'd known he was having trouble but didn't comprehend the full depth of what he'd lost. Not only his sister and his first love, but his entire life up until the present spent consumed by the past, the need to return to places that were as lost as he was. He left them with the journal and the decision that they would have to make. He apologized for not being surer of what he'd done before bringing them in. If they stayed, Arielle would eventually fade from them, sooner rather than later because he'd drawn her only months before she was to get sick.

They wrestled with the decision for days before going to their daughter. Arielle sat on the bed, journal in hand, writing about the things that were going on. It was a new journal, green instead of pink, bought at the local pharmacy.

"Things here are strange. I find it weird that I can hear everything Jonathan is thinking. Bailey explained to me why that was, but I still find it unsettling. I don't really know what I am here, or who I am. I'm not sure if I'm alive or dead. I feel real enough but don't know if that's just Jonathan or if it's me. I know that mom and dad are thinking about leaving, as is Jonathan, but what has me worried is if they go, what will happen here? Will I continue on or will I blink out again?"

The bedroom door opened and her parent's entered. She knew what they were going to say before they said it, the strange telepathy in this world made that possible and she could see what it was they truly wanted to do. They didn't want to stay with her if she wasn't her, but what they didn't seem to understand was that she was her. Something made that apparent to her. However, she knew that their staying wouldn't work. It was a temporary solution.

After two weeks of going back and forth, talking, crying, processing, they decided that it would be best to return to the real world. There was no guarantee that anything would continue and so to stay would be to delay the inevitable.

Jonathan sat on his bed, Emily asleep beside him. She had taken the news better than the others; it was never her intention to cross over. She was worried about the baby and what effect the new environment may be having on it. Jonathan believed he'd solved the problems of his life by creating this place and now he saw he had done nothing but caused more confusion. What pained him the most was the look on Arielle's face when he told her they'd be leaving.

He'd made a point to be the one to convey the news, knowing her thoughts might pass into her parents if they were the ones to do it. The pain that came was so heavy he'd been overwhelmed. Both he and Arielle sat together on the bed, tears from a million days spilling down both their cheeks. Jonathan could feel the parts of her that weren't connected to him and found solace in the thoughts he didn't recognize; her thoughts.

"Jonathan?" It was her voice.

He raised his head and looked at her. "What will happen when you go?"

"What do you mean?"

"Will this place stay? Will I stay?"

For a moment he didn't speak. "I don't know."

"I don't want to be here alone."

The words fell upon him breaking any sense he'd held of getting through it without hurting her. Jonathan felt a hate for himself so intense she had to put a hand on his to stop the trembling.

"It's okay." She said, trying to be strong.

"No, it's not. You shouldn't have to stay here alone."

"Its okay, you were just trying to help mama and dad."

"No I wasn't. I did it for myself, just like Bailey said. I was so selfish in not wanting to hurt anymore, I gave my hurt to everybody else."

"You didn't mean to."

"It doesn't matter whether I meant to or not, I did, and now it's worse than before."

"Jonathan, what's done is done. We can't go back and change it, we can only do the best we can with where we are."

"But its my fault." He said, trying to find some ember of hope in her.

"You couldn't have known."

He began to cry against her. She stroked the back of his head, whispering that it would be okay, trying to be strong against her own emotions threatening to break her down. When he got himself under control, he sat with her in the dark marking every piece of the scene. He would experience the moment now, but would not try to hold on to it. As the sun brought morning she slept, the perfect lines of her face reminding him of times lost and memories sweeter than life itself.

# Chapter Twenty-Eight

It was a beautiful day, a fitting end to such a somber evening. Arielle stood on the porch with him, careful not to interact with her mother and father until he had left. The strange appearance of her changing frightened Jonathan but it actually caused her pain. The attempt of two perceptions trying to gain hold made her head ache and her heart race.

Jonathan had spent the morning reopening the doorway and making sure it was still working correctly. He'd tried to use the doorway into their place and found it would not open. It helped cement the fact that the initial doors opened into the real world.

The door to his parent's bedroom was still intact and opened with the completion of the white space he'd introduced. He stepped through first making sure nothing would go wrong. He came out into the familiar smell of the room, realizing the smell was different here, it was natural. He walked to their bedroom window and looked out, the world still brightening with the day. The streets were lined with the cracked concrete he remembered, the houses lining the streets wore their ages. Crossing back through, he found Emily waiting for him.

"Safe?" She asked.

"Safe. You can head on through if you want."

She did, walking out of his world into the shared one.

Jonathan turned to his parents. "Is everything ready?"

"Yes, whenever you're ready."

"Don't push us through this time." His father said, doing his best to smile.

"I won't, promise."

They moved past him, knowing there would be no easier way than to just do it. They crossed through, entering their bedroom and feeling a strange sense of normalcy wash over them. Jonathan turned, meaning to go to Arielle one last time, but Bailey called him over.

He stood smoking his signature cigar, smiling as one does when seeing an old friend. "Today's the big day, huh?"

"Yeah."

"Everybody leaving?"

"Well, everybody but you and Arielle."

Bailey nodded and motioned towards her. "What does she think about that?"

"She's okay with it I guess."

"Doesn't seem okay to me."

"Well, she's scared of what will happen once I leave."

"Everything here stops."

Jonathan continued to look at his sister. "Are you sure?"

"Sure as I can be, every time I came back and went back none of the inhabitants remembered me leaving. They said it was as though I'd walked through the door then turned around and walked back in. I'm surprised you didn't read that."

"I must have missed it."

Bailey blew smoked into the air, "Yup, must have."

Jonathan looked at him. "I don't remember you mentioning anything about that in the journal, I read every page."

"Every page of which one?"

Jonathan was dumbfounded. "There are others? The one I read said you were moving on with your life."

"There are more."

"Why didn't you tell me about them?"

"Time wasn't right."

"Is it right now?"

"Feels like it might be."

"Where are they?"

"I left this particular one with her." And he nodded towards Arielle. "Told her not to read it though, she said she wouldn't."

"How long is it?"

"A few hundred pages."

"Well I don't have time to read that, besides, I've given up on all this, there's nothing in there that I care about."

"Maybe there is. I have the page marked for you. You let me know how interesting it is."

Jonathan looked at the man, the white smoke from his cigar dancing around his face, and thought again how little he truly knew him.

# Chapter Twenty-Nine

Bailey's Journal Page 133:
The Theory of Crossing Over

"Discovered something strange today, I've been going back through my notes and realized that I may have been wrong on one of my major points. While everything I've said about this world up until this point is true, particularly that the inhabitants within are dictated by the laws of which I've already concluded, today something has occurred which brings to light an interesting possibility.

As I've said before, I'd given up the study of

inhabitants. There were too many uncertainties to consider and I've spent most of this series of experiments looking at inanimate things, old trucks, antiques and such but it never dawned on me until now that there may be more here then I first believed.

If the theory holds true, that all within the perceived world exists on a plane designated by our first coming into contact with and then losing things, then those things have a beginning and an end determined by the time we had spent with them. What I noticed is that what I've brought out, be it a picture, or an old bucket, the thing continues to exist well beyond when it would have otherwise vacated. It leads me to an interesting possibility. What if what I perceive, when brought to this world, ceases to be a perception and becomes something tangible, something not of my making? At this point, the perception would become its own reflector therefore retaining its own sense of self within the plane of solidity.

I look at it like a painting, the basic premise of the whole argument. I have something inside of me, a need to create. Now, with that need I enlist the help of a medium in this case, canvas, paint, and powder. Then I proceed to create. When I finish this task I have made a thing that before only existed inside of me. Whereas I move into the painting I find that I move into myself, but on the other side, when looking at the painting, what I see is the thing itself. When I brought things out, I brought them out of me into the real world and by doing so I created them. I made them reality. The ramifications of this are astounding.

I have begun preliminary experiments and the results have been nothing short of amazing. "

Jonathan stopped reading, the realization of what had been offered to him enormous. Arielle was looking at him concerned. When he looked up at her she asked, "What does it say? And that was the question wasn't it? What did it say? He understood what it was trying to say, knew that if this particular piece of the puzzle was real then everything might not be lost after all. He turned to find Bailey standing with him, the old man looking down at the words he'd written.

"Seems kinda funny doesn't it?"

Jonathan could only look at him.

"It's so simple we miss what's in front of us."

"What do you mean?"

"How long have you tried to go back to her? How long have you been trying to get back to where you felt alive and free? The inherent problem I realized was that we can't go back to where we were, at least not forever. It's okay to visit for awhile, but you can't stay in the past, nothing but death back there. But if you can go back, figure out what it was that made you feel alive, then perhaps, just perhaps, you can bring that forward with you."

Jonathan's eyes blazed. "Are you saying..?"

"Why don't you give it a shot and see?"

Jonathan didn't move. It seemed so implausible and yet there was a truth to it. He turned to Bailey. "What about you?"

The man took another puff of his cigar and let the smoke drift. "I'll be right behind you."

They directed their attention towards Arielle who was looking confused at both of them. Jonathan took her hand, the emotions already trying to rob him of his voice. "I need you to come with me, Arielle."

She looked mistrustfully at him, "come with you where?"

"Through the door."

"What difference will that make? I don't exist there anymore. I'm part of this place, part of you."

"Just come with me."

"I'm scared."

Bailey leaned down to her ear and whispered, "fear is what keeps us still."

She gripped Jonathan's hand and stepped off the porch. They crossed the yard. Jonathan could already feel himself leaving this place behind, this world of lunatic memories and lost emotions. He could see his parents through the door, saw Emily sitting on the bed, and smelled the strange familiarity of the world he was born in.

As they crossed the threshold Arielle's grip on him tightened. Bailey crossed through behind them, pulling the door as he came. The rushing air slammed it shut. Arielle stood next to Jonathan, her mother and father both looking at her, and she realized something. She couldn't hear what they were thinking, nor could they hear her. Jonathan registered the change.

He felt a tap on his shoulder and turned.

"Well boy, looks like you made it through."

Jonathan nodded. "Yeah, looks like we all did."

Bailey smiled. "Yes, I usually do."

Arielle went to her mother, falling into her arms and crying. It was different now, it was real, and everyone knew it.

Jonathan turned to Bailey. "You knew all along didn't you?"

Bailey nodded. "Yes."

"Why didn't you just help me earlier?"

The question usually came after this part, first with the questions and then with the resolution, and none understanding, even after all that they'd seen.

"Let's just say that you needed to grow to understand. If you grow to understand before I have to intervene then so be it."

"You're not making any sense."

"An instrument must be understood before it is used or it is apt to be dangerous."

"But you were unskilled."

"Yes, and very dangerous."

"But you learned."

"Yes, through evils I would never allow you to see, I learned. But that is not what you want to ask me."

Jonathan looked at his mother and father, looked at his sister who had come back from inside of him, then looked back at Bailey.

"How many people have you brought out?"

"Ah, now there's an interesting question. Let's just say I've passed through that door a time or two."

"Was Camille the first?"

"I never brought her back."

"But she was the one who gave you the jars."

"Was she now?" And he laughed. In it, Jonathan

was unsure of everything. "How long have there been artists in the world Jonathan?"

"Since forever I would think."

"Yes, and what about the magic?"

"Just as long?"

"Was it coincidence that Camille's mother had this powder? Perhaps. Was it coincidence that I recognized it for what it was? Perhaps. But I couldn't tell her you see. I knew where she was going, and I knew how to create it. In fact, the farm itself, my mother and father, all of them, were of my creation."

Jonathan stared at him and Bailey smiled. "I knew Camille would come, I had heard her cries many times while exploring the lands beyond, and I knew she would come. Some of us aren't meant to be where we are."

Jonathan felt his head swimming.

"When I was a boy, born to the world and truly your age, I was brought by my father to a man whose name you would recognize. Under his watchful eye I became a skilled painter. It was he who gave me the secret of the powder and taught me of true creation."

The old man reached in his shirt pocket and found a cigar. "Let me ask you, what is it that you see when you look around? What is that feeling that overtakes you when you allow something inside of your mind. That sensation of lunatic need. Do you see beauty? If so, how do you know beauty? Where have you seen it before? Why must you quench the need to filter your mind onto the page. Where did you learn that?

These were the questions he posed to me, and that I now pose to you."

Jonathan looked at his old friend, understanding enough of what he was saying to send chills down his spine.

"I will leave you a small amount of the powder, enough that you will be careful of its use and not waste it. The rest I'm taking with me. My part of your education is over. You have passed the test with flying colors. You now must take some time to understand what it is you are and what path you must take to fulfill your responsibility here. The others will never understand you, and you can never explain to them what it is you feel. Only go with the knowledge that nothing here is real and one day the layers will be peeled back. Until then, you and I are parted. It's been good growing with you." With it said Bailey turned and walked out the door. Jonathan watched him go.

Emily hadn't heard everything, but had heard enough to understand that things for her and Jonathan would never be the same. The prospect of the boy she loved was stranger now than ever, but she would never leave his side again.

"Jonathan?"

He turned to her.

"I love you."

He smiled and sat down next to her, his hand going to her stomach, "I love you too."

"Thank you." She said.

"For what?"

"For bringing me home."

## JEREMY RANDOLPH

Arielle sat with her mother and his father on the bed, the same bed where so many times both she and Jonathan had run from the fear of nightmares to the comfort of things greater than their fear, snuggling into the warmth of the covers and the closeness of being part of something, of being safe.

# Chapter Thirty

Bailey Hazelwood stopped by Jonathan's room and plucked the picture of the jars from his wall. He could hear the laughter and the conversations as he moved through the house. They'd already begun to find their old rhythm, and he knew before long they would be lost in its numbing walls. Even with all they'd seen, most would seek the shelter of oblivion because to know what truth lay beyond left nothing in the mind but misery, anger and eventual madness. He couldn't blame them for what they were, nor could he punish them for not seeing. Master Jonathan might hold on to the things that he'd learned, but when given back the thing you long for you find the driving force which propelled you to your understanding no longer held the potency needed.

As night fell he checked himself into a hotel and finished a beautiful portrait of his sister, Abigail. He brought her back into the world; the shadowy portion of Alzheimer's nowhere to be found.

"How long was I gone this time?" She asked.

Bailey calculated, fiddling with a matchbook. "At least a year."

She considered this. "That's not bad, not like the last time. How long was that one?"

Bailey set the matchbook down and turned on the television. "Seventeen years."

"Oh yes, seventeen. My, that's a long time."

"I wasn't sure we'd come back this time, I thought the boy would give up."

Abigail picked up her brush and began to comb her hair. "Well you have a way of keeping them interested."

"Yes, I suppose so. I'm just glad I was able to show him what he needed to see. Too many are lost to the truth."

"Some choose not to see it."

"Maybe I didn't show them enough."

"Those were not your fault."

"I delivered them into it."

"They delivered themselves, Bailey."

"Perhaps. I died this time did I tell you?"

"You did?"

"Yes."

"Then it really was close." She stopped brushing

and turned to him. "What did you see in the dark?

He closed his eyes and saw what he had seen, a deep fear permiating through him. "I'd rather not say."

Abigail looked at him. "They will catch us eventually."

Bailey nodded. "I know, but for now we're safe."

"Yes," she agreed, "for now."

She went back to brushing her hair, the soft auburn hues painted the beloved texture he always associated with her, perfect in every strand.

They were gone before the sun rose, heading west towards California. Morning Ridge fell away, another closed chapter in their haunted lives. Abigail began singing, a song she learned years before, the words soft in the small interior of the car. He joined in with Abbey, the sounds of their voices disappearing into the hum of the highway. "Let us all be free, from tomorrow and today, for all that I have loved, dear Lord, has long since passed away."

OTHER BOOKS BY JEREMY RANDOLPH

*CIRCA*

*BORDERLANDS*

*www.JeremyRandolph.com*

*Visit Us Online At:*

*WinterNightPublishing.com*